If the l...

She'll live...

In these contemporary twists on classic fairy tales from Harlequin Romance, allow yourself to be swept away on a jet-set adventure where the modern-day heroine is the star of the story. The journey toward happy-ever-after may not be easy, but in a land far away, true love will *always* result in their dreams coming true—especially with a little help from Prince Charming!

Get lost in the magic of...

Their Fairy Tale India Escape
by Ruby Basu

Part of His Royal World
by Nina Singh

Cinderella's Billion-Dollar Invitation
by Michele Renae

Beauty and the Playboy Prince
by Justine Lewis

All available now!

Dear Reader,

I have always loved fairy tales, so when my editor asked if I'd be interested in writing a modern retelling, of course I jumped at the chance.

There is something about fairy tales that is universal. There are similar stories in many different cultures and they transcend time. For me, this is what makes modern retellings so exciting.

Of course, the stories change and adapt. Thankfully! I remember reading the original tales by the Brothers Grimm and wondering whether I was mistranslating the stories because they were so different from the ones I'd heard growing up—for good reason. But many tales share fundamental themes of family and love. And that's certainly true in Rina and Connor's story.

Rina and Connor both had unusual upbringings, which made them the people they are at the beginning of the story. Connor is closed off and doesn't like getting close to people, whereas Rina yearns to make connections. As they spend time together in Bengaluru, Mysuru and Mumbai, they grow closer. But they both need to learn how to defeat the metaphorical dragons that keep them apart before they can have their happy ending.

I hope you enjoy reading my *Rapunzel* retelling.

Love,

Ruby

Their Fairy Tale India Escape

Ruby Basu

If you purchased this book without a cover you should be aware that this book is stolen property. It was reported as "unsold and destroyed" to the publisher, and neither the author nor the publisher has received any payment for this "stripped book."

HARLEQUIN®
Romance™

Recycling programs for this product may not exist in your area.

ISBN-13: 978-1-335-59656-7

Their Fairy Tale India Escape

Copyright © 2024 by Ruby Basu

All rights reserved. No part of this book may be used or reproduced in any manner whatsoever without written permission except in the case of brief quotations embodied in critical articles and reviews.

This is a work of fiction. Names, characters, places and incidents are either the product of the author's imagination or are used fictitiously. Any resemblance to actual persons, living or dead, businesses, companies, events or locales is entirely coincidental.

For questions and comments about the quality of this book, please contact us at CustomerService@Harlequin.com.

Harlequin Enterprises ULC
22 Adelaide St. West, 41st Floor
Toronto, Ontario M5H 4E3, Canada
www.Harlequin.com

Printed in U.S.A.

Ruby Basu lives in the beautiful Chilterns with her husband, two children and the cutest dog in the world. She worked for many years as a lawyer and policy lead in the Civil Service. As the second of four children, Ruby connected strongly with *Little Women*'s Jo March and was scribbling down stories from a young age. She loves creating new characters and worlds.

Books by Ruby Basu

Harlequin Romance

Baby Surprise for the Millionaire
Cinderella's Forbidden Prince
Sailing to Singapore with the Tycoon

Visit the Author Profile page
at Harlequin.com.

To Pixy, the Beth to my Jo.

**Praise for
Ruby Basu**

"Absolutely lovely Cinderella romance with a
wonderful setting... It's tropetastic but a good
trope well deployed is a wonderful thing and this
is beautifully done. Assured writing, charming
characters, involving tale...and generally an
excellent book if you just need to exhale."

—Author KJ Charles via *Goodreads*
on *Cinderella's Forbidden Prince*

CHAPTER ONE

CONNOR PORTLAND STOPPED his car at the end of the road—or what he'd been calling a road. He'd been driving up hills along what was effectively a dirt track for the last few miles, but now even that had become too small to support much more than a bike. At the side of the track, the grass had been cleared, whether intentionally or by constant use, and looked like somewhere he could park safely without risking his tyres getting stuck.

He got out of his car and started to walk along the path, barely noticing the incline as he looked around him at the fields of purple plants and, further in the distance, the mountains surrounding Lake Thun.

As he continued walking, what looked like a mini castle came into view, with a medieval-looking stone building in between two bergfried towers, one square and the other circular.

Although it was the only building for miles,

the castle blended seamlessly into the picturesque surroundings. Nobody looking at the fairy tale building would imagine it was the living and working premises of Lachance Boutique, an up-and-coming haircare brand. How could such an unusual building have developed Essence, by Lachance, loved by people who knew and used it and proclaimed by them as a miracle haircare product—and the reason he was in the area.

His phone rang, almost surprising him. In the vast quietness of his surroundings he had forgotten about things like mobile phone reception. He answered the call, then listened to his assistant's latest update. It was no surprise to hear that she'd managed to rearrange his flights and hotels to accommodate his meeting with Lachance.

He had planned to leave the following day, for his next site visit to Munich, and then spend a couple of days back in England, taking a break. Perhaps visiting his brother and sister, before heading out to India for a week or so. Now it sounded as if the best solution would be to rearrange his plans and remain in Switzerland, drive from there to Munich, and go straight on to India after that. He would have to give up his intended break, but that was nothing new. He didn't mind working—it was the constant travelling he tried to avoid.

Usually, once he'd started his annual inspections, travelling round to various offices and distribution centres in Europe, he preferred to keep going—if he had to live out a suitcase he would rather get it over and done with.

He briskly gave his assistant some further instructions before ending the call. He looked around again at the view. What was he even doing here?

Not usually an impulsive man, instead of returning to his hotel in Geneva, Connor had driven to this small village in Sigriswil, where Lachance Boutique was based. Was he hoping that by spending some time in the area he would be able to find out more about the brand? There was very little research available online.

It was a small family company, which had somehow managed to develop a once-in-a-lifetime product that many companies were desperate to get their hands on. He already knew some of his usual competitors had approached Lachance with deals which had been firmly rejected.

His company's potential deal with Lachance Boutique wouldn't be make-or-break for his company from a financial perspective—it was too large and successful for that to be a concern. From a personal perspective, though, it would be a massive step in the right direction towards a promotion from Director of European Operations to Global CEO. And promotion meant more responsibility, more money and no more business travel.

In some ways the prospect of no longer travelling for work was more attractive than the financial package and new challenges the promotion would bring.

Connor had spent his childhood moving from town to town, following his father from one job to the next. His family had moved to wherever his father could find work, although he never seemed able to keep any job for long. Sometimes Connor had felt his father didn't even try to stay in one place. That wasn't what Connor wanted for his life. He was content living in London—where he could be there to support his brother and sister while his parents continued moving, travelling round the world rather than being restricted to Great Britain, now he and his siblings had left home.

Unfortunately this change of plan meant he wouldn't have time to spend with his siblings, but they probably wouldn't mind—it wasn't the first time work had to come first. The greater shame was he wouldn't be able to fit in a trip to Adysara, to catch up with his old university friend Rohan.

A movement in one of the higher fields caught his attention. He narrowed his eyes to bring the figure into focus. He could make out a small, slim woman. He watched as the woman reached up and loosened her bun, his eyes widening as long, luxuriant black hair flowed down her back. Even from a distance he could tell the length was touching her waist.

He huffed out a laugh as the wind caught her hair and threw it about her face, watching her fight against the flying strands. He had never cared much about people's hair before, but found himself tensing up when she gathered her hair behind her, hoping she wasn't going to put it back into the bun. He relaxed when he saw she was twisting the strands into a long braid.

There was something familiar about her. Could she be the woman he'd noticed the previous evening? He'd stopped for a meal in the village, before driving on to his hotel. As he'd left the restaurant he'd heard a joyous peal of laughter and instinctively sought out where the sound was coming from. She'd been standing next to an older woman who was opening the door to a house. The only illumination had come from the porch light, but he'd been able to make out her huge smile even at that distance.

With hair like that, she had to use Lachance products. But for some reason work was the last thing he wanted to think about when he looked at her.

Without really understanding why, he walked in her direction.

Rina Lachance sighed deeply as she lay in the field of rampion and gazed up at the cloudless sky. Another frustrating day in the lab. She didn't mind the repetitive task of distilling the essential liquids needed to create their signature products, but she hadn't come up with any new products for almost half a year. Where was her inspiration…her creativity?

She watched as a cloud shaped like a lion slowly floated across the sky. She was sure she'd seen that exact cloud passing before. She'd been staring up at the same sky for the past sixteen years, ever since she'd come to Switzerland to live with Aunt Maria after her parents had died.

There was such a lot of world covered by that same sky and she'd seen so little of it.

For a brief moment Rina allowed herself to imagine what her life would have been like if that terrible car accident had never happened. Would she have travelled more? She'd seen photos of herself when she was very young, posing with her parents in front of various tourist attractions in Italy, Greece and Peru, but she couldn't remember going to any of them.

She could barely remember her parents.

She had very few memories of her childhood before moving to Switzerland.

According to Aunt Maria, her doctors had said it wasn't unusual for someone who had been through a traumatic experience to try to block out painful memories.

Rina sometimes wondered whether she'd inherited her mother's sense of adventure. Her mother had moved from India to England when she was ten, and then, while at university, had spent a year studying in Switzerland—which was where she'd met Rina's father.

Rina had moved to Switzerland when she was ten and she hadn't gone anywhere out of the country since then. She'd barely left her village.

She expelled a breath of frustration. What was the point of thinking about what might have been and where she might have vis-

ited? Her aunt would never let her leave Lachance tower. Rina had suggested they travel
together, to get new ideas for products, but
her aunt wouldn't go. There was nothing she
could think of to say that would persuade
Aunt Maria that nothing serious would happen to her if they went abroad.

Rina stretched out an arm to her side, strok-
ing the purple petals of the flowers. There
was only so much she could do with the liquid she extracted from these plants. Even if
she came up with a new method of extraction
there wouldn't be any significant difference
in the end product.

Essence, by Lachance, had taken off in a
way Rina could never have imagined. Her initial goal had been rather self-serving—she'd
wanted to create a product that could tame her
own wild mane. But, although their distribution channels had been small, the amazing
effects of the product had spread by word of
mouth, with many companies offering to buy
the product or be granted a licence to produce
it. So far her aunt had turned down every
proposal and, if Rina was honest, she hadn't
been particularly interested in any of the offers they'd had so far. Even the companies
that were prepared to accept a licence rather
than buying Essence outright wanted their

licence to be exclusive. And they wanted to keep the product exclusive too—which meant it would be out of the budgets of most people Rina wanted to help.

Rina had hoped that the success of Essence might lead to opportunities for her to leave Lake Thun and finally travel the world, but her aunt was happy to maintain the status quo.

If only she knew what words could convince Aunt Maria that she needed more...

Rina needed to get away. She was feeling more and more stifled every day. There was so much to do outside their village, but she didn't think she could leave if it would make Aunt Maria unhappy. Rina could never disappoint her aunt—she owed everything to her. Aunt Maria had happily taken her in and raised Rina after her parents had died.

And, in the circumstances, Rina understood why her aunt was so overprotective of her. Aunt Maria had lost her fiancé in the accident which had killed her brother and Rina's mother. She had stayed by Rina's hospital bed for almost a year, as she'd recovered from brain injuries which had seen her in a medically induced coma and then had undergone extensive physical rehabilitation. Aunt Maria had occasional panic attacks since the accident, which was part of the reason she preferred staying close to home. Although her aunt had made Rina take counselling after the accident, Rina had never managed to persuade her aunt to do the same, and every time she mentioned it even now she knew she was beating her head against the wall.

Rina wished she could persuade her aunt that she was fully recovered, but she still had the occasional headache—which caused her aunt's anxiety to heighten.

No, she couldn't leave, knowing how much it would upset her aunt. But every day it was getting harder to stay.

CHAPTER TWO

RINA'S WATCH BEEPED. She sat up. Only twenty minutes of her break left and she still had to eat. She brought her braid over her shoulder, to make sure there weren't any leaves caught in it, and as she stood up she noticed a man standing next to a tree, staring out over the view of the lake.

She didn't blame him—she often stood in the same position, taking everything in. But he clearly wasn't local. She recognised everyone in the nearest village—there weren't many of them, and people rarely moved into the area. It was a popular area for hikes, but it was unusual for tourists to be on their own—they were usually part of a walking group. Perhaps he had got separated from his companions...

She approached him slowly.

'Are you lost?' she asked.

There was no response. She tilted her head. It was possible he didn't understand German, so she repeated her question in French and English.

Rina sucked in a breath when the man turned round.

Oh, he's finally here! she thought.

But she didn't know where that idea had come from. She wasn't expecting him—she wasn't expecting anyone. And she'd never seen him before, despite that inner sense of recognition. If they'd previously met there was no way she would have forgotten him.

He looked like a romance book hero, with his dark blond, almost brown hair lifting in the breeze across his forehead. His eyes were a startling green, their colour so vivid they looked as if they came from a child's painting. She'd never seen anyone with that colour eyes in real life before.

She put her hand to her chest—had her heart actually skipped a beat?

As he observed her he blinked, then did a double take.

What had caused his reaction? Perhaps she had flowers and twigs in her hair. She resisted the urge to check her braid again, and willed herself to stand still under his silent examination.

'Sorry, I was miles away. What did you say?' he asked when he finally spoke.

At least now she knew he spoke English. Luckily she spoke all three languages equally fluently.

'I asked if you're lost,' she repeated. 'This path won't lead anywhere but more hills and fields.'

He shook his head. 'I'm just taking a stroll.'

Rina looked back at the path he must have used. It wasn't the gentlest incline. She glanced down at his shoes. They were sturdy, but not the usual choice for people planning to walk for miles. She looked over his casual clothes, momentarily distracted by his strong forearms which were displayed by the shirt-sleeves he'd rolled to his elbows. Again, although he wasn't wearing the kind of clothes regular hikers chose, he was dressed in a similar way to many of the tourists who came to the area.

'You came to this area for a stroll?'

She tilted her head. Their village wasn't known as a tourist destination—and, unlike much of the area around Lake Thun, it had very little of interest.

'I came down yesterday from Geneva. I passed through this area on my way to my hotel and wanted to see if it was as beautiful in the daytime,' he explained.

She supposed that made sense. She had

half wondered if he had come to the area because of the company, but her aunt hadn't
mentioned any upcoming meetings so there
was no reason to suspect that. He turned to
the lake again, but she was sure he kept stealing glances at her.

'And *is* it as beautiful in the daytime?' she
asked, her voice husky.

'Even more so,' he replied. 'Today I can
fully see the breathtaking lake, majestic
mountains, beautiful people… *Very* beautiful.'

Now there was no doubt he was looking
at her.

Her throat went dry. Were they flirting
with each other? She had to admit there had
been a flirtatious tone to her question, and
she was delighted he'd reciprocated. A brief
flirtation with a handsome stranger would
be the perfect antidote to her humdrum days.

She was trying to think of something witty
to say when he surprised her by asking if she
lived in the area. She nodded.

'I had dinner in the village restaurant. You
live in the house opposite it, don't you?'

Rina didn't reply. She didn't want to lie
to him, but she didn't want to mention the
tower. Even tourists had heard of Lachance,
and often treated her like some kind of genius when they found out she developed all

the products—she didn't want to risk opening that line of conversation. She *had* been
in town the previous evening, for her regular catch-up with one of the residents. It was
possible he'd seen her.

He held up his hand to stop her replying.
'I'm sorry, that was too personal,' he said.

Her eyes widened at this interpretation
of her reluctance to reply. Aunt Maria had
drummed into her the fact that she needed to
be careful about the information she shared
with other people. Her aunt always claimed
Rina was too trusting, but she knew it was really because of her aunt's overprotectiveness.
Although she had to admit it hadn't crossed
her mind that he'd been 'too personal'.

'I could promise you I'm not a stalker—but
I'm sure that's what a stalker would say,' he
continued, his face widening into a big grin
which crinkled the corners of his eyes and
made him look younger and very approach-
able.

Rina couldn't help returning his grin.

The previous evening she had noticed a
large figure leaving the restaurant, but she
hadn't been able to see his face. Staring at
him now, she thought that was probably a
good thing, or she was certain his handsome
features would have pervaded her dreams.

She hadn't felt this kind of attraction before. It was making her have unrealistic thoughts—such as trying to come up with reasons to spend time with him. And she didn't even know his name.

'Do you know anything about that tower over there? The receptionist at my hotel mentioned it. It's unusual.'

He nodded in the direction of her home.

Rina smiled. 'Of course. Everyone in the area knows about Lachance Tower. But unfortunately you can't take tours of it. It's a family home and business—not for tourists. It was constructed to be a mini replica of Oberhofen Castle on the shore of Lake Thun. Have you seen it? It has a museum too.'

He shook his head. 'I haven't, but it sounds interesting.'

'I could show you around if you're not familiar with the area?'

She tried to sound nonchalant as she made her offer—she'd made similar offers to previous visitors she'd come across—but this was the first time she knew she'd be disappointed if he refused.

There was a brief flare in his eyes. Was it surprise or interest? She was too much of a novice at male-female interactions to interpret it properly.

Instead of responding to her offer he said, 'I'm Connor Portland,' and put out his hand.

Rina gave it a quick clasp, knowing that if she held on longer than a moment she would be reluctant to let go. She'd never felt such an intense reaction to someone before.

'Pleased to meet you, Connor,' she replied. 'I'm Rina La—' She cleared her throat, managing to remember at the last minute Aunt Maria's warnings about giving strangers too much information about herself, particularly when she had such a distinctive name. Instead, she used her mother's maiden name. 'Rina Lahiri.'

'You must find it very peaceful out here, Rina,' Connor said, briefly glancing around him before turning back to stare at her.

She shrugged and gave a rueful smile. 'Not much traffic. You said you came down from Geneva. Is that where you live?'

He shook his head. 'London. I was in Geneva on business.'

Rina felt a pang of envy. Having the chance to travel for work was something she dreamed of.

'Do you come to Switzerland a lot?' she asked, knowing her question wasn't solely out of politeness.

'Not really. Once or twice a year.'

She couldn't help feeling disappointed in his answer. Her reaction was disproportionate, considering she'd only met him a few minutes before and they had hardly had the most riveting conversation.

'Do you travel much?'

His lips formed a thin line. 'More than I'd like.'

She couldn't imagine anyone not enjoying the chance to explore different countries. But perhaps he had someone at home he didn't like being away from.

'Where do you usually travel?'

'Usually Europe and the States although I occasionally go further afield if I need to.'

'Really? Have you ever been to Japan or Brazil?'

'I've been to Japan on business. But not Brazil.'

'What about for pleasure? Do you go abroad on holiday?'

He furrowed his brow. She supposed she was asking an unusual number of questions about travel to a complete stranger, but as someone who'd spent practically her entire life in one place, she could only live vicariously through the experiences of others.

'I only travel when strictly necessary.'

She wasn't sure whether his short response

was because travelling was somehow un-
pleasant for him or whether it was because
he didn't want to continue the conversation.

'You're very lucky,' she said in a subdued
tone.

'I *am* lucky,' he replied, but she got the impression he wasn't talking about travel.

He had an unusual smile on his face, as
if he was thinking of a secret joke, when he
took a step closer to her and reached towards
her. She froze for a second, hardly daring to
breathe. Was he going to kiss her?

She felt foolish and also disappointed when
he reached up to her head instead.

'You have something in your hair,' he said,
holding out a purple flower.

She blinked, certain she hadn't imagined
the sensation of a caress along her hair as he'd
pulled out the flower.

'What is this?' he asked, 'It's very pretty.'

'It's rampion. Rampion bellflower.'

'I've heard of rampion. I hadn't seen it
before, though.' He looked around over the
fields full of the plant.

He'd heard of rampion? Rina narrowed her
eyes. Could he possibly know about Essence,
by Lachance? Many of the businesses that
had offered to buy her formula had tried re-
verse engineering the product, and they knew

a key ingredient was rampion, although they didn't know about the unique extraction technique that made Essence so effective.

She couldn't deny Connor interested her—a lot—and she wanted to find out as much as she could about him. But suddenly she didn't want to know why he was in the area or what he did for work. Because everything would change if he was in the area because he wanted to do business with Lachance Boutique.

She inwardly rolled her eyes. Now she was thinking like Aunt Maria, suspecting that everyone she met had ulterior motives. He'd told her he was in the area for a stroll, and if he already knew about Lachance Boutique he wouldn't be so curious about the tower.

She changed the conversation and told him more about the area and the other places of interest nearby. He was leaning back, resting his elbows against the fence, his pose perfectly casual, but she could tell he was paying attention to her from his astute questions and observations.

She didn't know whether to look at his face or at his relaxed figure—both were too distracting for her peace of mind. She wanted to spend more time with Connor and get to know him better, for however long he was in the area, but she didn't even know how long that would be.

'It sounds like I will need a tour guide to get the most out of my visit,' Connor said, when Rina finally ran out of places to mention.

There was something in his tone that made her heart beat a little faster. Did he want to spend more time with her?

'I can show you around. Will your wife or family be joining us?' She grimaced—her question had not been subtle at all.

His mouth quirked. 'I'm on my own.'

She tried to contain her grin. 'I can meet you tomorrow.'

'Are you sure you aren't busy?'

'I'm on holiday,' she replied.

It wasn't true. In fact she hardly ever took any real time off work. But, apart from being surprised, she doubted her colleagues would care. Her aunt would be another matter, though.

'Do you work round here, then? What do you do?'

'I help out my aunt.'

Hopefully, her aunt would approve of the vagueness of that answer.

He nodded, but didn't ask her to expand.

'How long are you in the area? I can plan

out the best itinerary for however many days you have.'

He didn't reply immediately. She could almost see the thoughts flashing through his brain as he worked out actions, consequences and rationale.

Had he ever tried just living in the moment? Or was he, like her, prevented from giving in to whims and impulsive actions by what he owed other people. Did they share that in common?

'Two days,' he said finally, flashing her another flirtatious grin that made her breath catch. 'You can play my tourist guide for both days if you're free.'

She clapped her hands like a sea lion after performing a trick.

'Perfect,' she replied. 'Why don't we meet tomorrow on the Sigriswil Panoramic Bridge? That's a great place to start our tour and easy to find.' She glanced at her watch. 'I need to go now. But I'll see you there tomorrow. Ten o'clock? You'll be there won't you?'

She didn't know why it was so important to check—she just knew she wanted to see him again.

He nodded. She expelled a breath, smiled brightly and walked away, giving him a small wave. She walked towards the lane, heading in the direction of the village rather than the tower. She closed her eyes briefly, imagining what her aunt's reaction would be when she told her she was taking a few mornings off and working out what reason she would give for her hasty action.

The only thing Rina knew for sure was that she didn't want her aunt to know about Connor. She was drawn to him in a way she hadn't experienced before and she didn't want anyone to ruin that feeling—especially not her suspicious aunt, who would never understand, and Rina couldn't explain, why she instinctively trusted him.

Connor would be her perfect secret.

Connor walked to his car, deliberately not turning to look behind him. He had a feeling if he caught a glimpse of Rina again he would not be able to stop himself returning to her, wanting to grasp a few more moments talking to her.

He'd been frustrated earlier, when he'd realised he'd lost track of the woman, but she must have been lying down in the field, based on the flowers in her hair. He couldn't explain the pleasure he'd felt when she'd approached him—beyond the basic pleasure of seeing a beautiful woman up close.

In some ways their conversation had been very standard—the kind of questions that strangers asked to get to know each other a little better. And yet it had felt far from ordinary.

What was it about Rina that kept him chatting, wanting to prolong their time together, even agreeing to meet her again to tour the area—something he'd had no intention of doing before she'd brought it up.

Before getting in his car, he pulled out his phone to call his assistant, informing her he would be taking the next couple of days off. It was unusual for him to take time off, particularly before an important presentation, but he knew his team was capable of finalising things, and he would be available for them if necessary.

He expelled a breath after he ended his call. He was acting completely out of character, rearranging his timetable so that he had the chance to meet Rina again—particularly when he knew a relationship with her was out of the question. It wasn't just the long distance; he didn't do relationships.

Moving around so much as child, he'd learnt not to get too close to anyone. There was never any point forming an attachment when he'd known he'd have to move on at short notice. He'd learnt that the hard way—ending friendships because his father had lost yet another job and the family had to move on. Soon, the necessity of saying goodbye had been the only certainty in his life.

The first time Connor had experienced any stability was during his undergraduate studies. Even with his disrupted schooling he'd demonstrated academic excellence from an early age, so when the time came to take national exams he'd performed well enough to get into the best university. But he'd never been sure where home would be during the holidays.

His younger brother and sister hadn't been so lucky. They had struggled with their education because his parents had suddenly decided they were going to home-school the two of them, which inevitably meant they were left to their own devices. Connor had tried to take their education into his hands, along with everything else, but he'd had to leave them when they insisted he go to university. He never forgot their sacrifice for him, encouraging him to pursue his education, so supporting them now by financing their homes was the least he could do in return.

He'd had girlfriends in the past—career women who understood his drive and passion for work—but none had ever lasted for more than a few months. He wasn't good at making commitments. His unstable childhood prevented him from getting too close to anyone, always prepared to pack up and move on. And he never wanted to lead anyone to believe there was a future with him when he knew that wasn't possible.

But he was getting ahead of himself. Just because he was interested in Rina didn't mean the interest was reciprocated. For all he knew Rina could be the kind of person who liked acting as a tour guide and wanted to do a good deed for a solo traveller.

He paused. He hadn't imagined the gleam of attraction when she had given him a once-over, nor her flirtatious responses to him.

First things first, he would return to his hotel and effectively put in two days' worth of work, so his team would be in the best possible position while he took time off to tour the area.

He shook his head with a laugh—he could hardly believe he was making all this trouble for himself just because he'd unexpectedly met a beautiful, interesting, intriguing woman he wanted to spend more time with. His gut instinct told him he wouldn't regret it.

What was it about Rina that captivated him

in the brief time they spent together? And even before they met, when he'd heard her laugh the previous evening? He could spend his time trying to analyse it, but he was only in the area for a couple of days. Instead he would enjoy getting to know her more... maybe leaning into their flirtatious behaviour.

And if their flirtation led to her offering a brief fling before he left Switzerland, then he wouldn't mind that at all.

CHAPTER THREE

RINA TWISTED HER braid as she walked up to their designated meeting spot in the car park near the Sigriswil Panoramic Bridge. She wasn't sure if she was worried Connor wouldn't be there or that he would.

She didn't know why she was so nervous. This wasn't the first time she'd acted as an unofficial tourist guide for visitors. But they had been families, or couples. Never an incredibly handsome single man. At least she assumed Connor was single. He hadn't specifically told her that, simply that he was here alone. For all she knew he could have a wife and family back in London.

Rina stumbled over the idea Connor might not be single. It shouldn't matter to her whether he was or not, but she really hoped he was. Surely he would never have flirted with her or agreed to meet with her again if he was in a committed relationship with someone else?

Why was she even thinking about Connor's relationship status? The only reason for it to bother her was if she was hoping that there was a possibility he was really interested in her, that he didn't flirt with every woman he met and imply they were beautiful.

She knew nothing would come of it—he lived in England, and she could never leave Aunt Maria or Switzerland. But that didn't mean she couldn't enjoy spending time in the company of the most gorgeous man she'd ever seen and find out more about all the travelling he did. She could hear about all the places she'd only dreamed of visiting.

And if he did happen to show he wanted something more with her, she would turn him down—firmly but politely.

But there was no way a plain, boring young woman who had barely left her own backyard could hold the interest of someone as handsome and sophisticated as Connor.

She sighed with relief when she saw Connor leaning next to a car up ahead. As she walked closer to him his features became clearer and stronger. She giggled—the uncontrollable giggle she gave when she saw celebrity photos of someone so good looking they didn't seem real. She'd wondered whether she had exaggerated how handsome he was in her memories. But she could see now she had not. And the image in her memories didn't even do justice to the sheer magnetism of his physical presence.

She quickened her pace to reach him.

'Hi, Connor.' She greeted him with a small wave.

She caught the twinkle in his eyes as she approached and his wide grin made his pleasure clear. Although it was a natural smile, she had a feeling his mouth wasn't used to stretching that much.

'Is there anywhere you particularly want to go?' she asked.

'Not really. I'm at your disposal.'

She cleared her throat at the inappropriate thoughts that came to her at the idea of having him truly at her disposal.

'Have you been across the suspension bridge yet?' she asked. When he shook his head, she gestured in front of her. 'Why don't we do that first? You're not afraid of heights, are you?'

'I don't think so.'

She bit her lip. 'Well, I can protect you if you do feel scared.'

His brow quirked, but he didn't reply as she

led the way to the start of the famous Sigriswil Panoramic Bridge.

Once they reached the middle of the bridge they stopped to take in the breathtaking views of Lake Thun and the surrounding mountains, and then looked down into the bottom of Gummischlucht gorge.

Connor commented on the surprising amount of tourists taking photos of the bridge itself rather than the views.

'This bridge became quite famous recently, because it was a filming spot for a very popular Korean drama,' Rina explained. 'Have you watched any Korean dramas?'

'I've watched a few, and some Korean films, but I don't remember watching one where this bridge features. Would you recommend it?'

She shrugged. 'I enjoyed it, but I don't really know what your tastes are.'

He gave her a small, almost shy smile. 'I hope you'll have a better idea once we've spent more time together.'

'I hope so too.' She cleared her throat. 'Would you like me to take a photo of you?' she offered.

Connor raised his eyebrows, as if he had never considered photos. Perhaps he wasn't someone who needed those kinds of reminders. If she ever got a chance to travel she would probably be so busy soaking up the atmosphere, trying to be present in the moment, she would also fail at taking photos to capture those memories.

Connor took his phone out of his pocket. 'Can I take a picture of you standing over there?'

Her eyes widened. Did he want a photo to remember her?

'To give a sense of scale,' he explained.

Something about the hurried way he spoke made her think that wasn't the real reason.

She gave him a nod, then went to stand where he indicated, feeling stiff and awkward.

'Smile!' Connor encouraged. 'You look like you're facing a firing squad.'

Rina laughed.

'That's more like it,' Connor said.

She didn't know how many pictures he snapped before he brought his phone down.

'Excuse me.' An older gentleman walking arm in arm with his wife spoke to them. 'Would you like us to take a photo of you both together?'

'That's not ne—' Rina began, but at the same time Connor spoke.

'Thanks. I'd appreciate that,' he said.

He gave his phone to the man, then came to stand next to her.

'Closer together,' the man instructed.

They both moved closer, bumping their sides. Rina gave a nervous laugh, which stopped abruptly when she felt Connor's arm around her.

The man took a few shots, then handed the phone back to Connor. Rina hurriedly passed her own phone to him—she wasn't going to miss the opportunity to have a photograph of her and Connor together.

After Connor had reciprocated the favour, by taking a few photos of the elderly couple, he indicated to Rina they should continue across the bridge.

He entwined her arm with his. 'This part looks high. I'm a little scared. You promised you'd protect me,' he said with a gleam.

'Of course,' she replied, even though there was no difference here from the height of the bridge they had already crossed.

Being close to Connor's side and soaking up his warmth made Rina feel as if she was the one being protected. She gave a slight sigh.

'Is everything all right?' Connor asked immediately.

'Oh, yes,' she replied, slightly surprised that

he'd been attuned to her enough to hear her small exhalation. 'It's breathtaking, isn't it?' she added, trying to give a reason.

'Very.'

Warmth flooded her cheeks when she noticed he was staring at her intently, not at the view. She tried to calm her erratic heartbeat.

'What's your favourite view?' she asked.

He barked a laugh. 'I'm not sure.'

'Tell me about some of the top views from your travels, then.'

He didn't have time to say much before they reached the other side of the bridge. At Rina's suggestion, they took a ferry to Thun, where they toured Schadau Castle before finding a restaurant for lunch.

At first Rina felt awkward, sitting down opposite Connor, looking directly at him. There had been less intensity when they were walking side by side. She kept hoping he would initiate some conversation, and when he didn't she looked around the room and out of the window. Each time they caught each other's glance they would smile, but say nothing. They'd talked about the area and the sights while they were walking, but now she wanted to get a chance to know more about Connor on a personal level.

She couldn't really ask him about his family, because then he would ask about hers, and when she explained she lived with her aunt it could lead to him discovering they were Lachances, and the Lachance name was too well known in the area for Connor not to understand its importance. She couldn't ask about his work, either, because that could encourage him to ask more about what she did for her aunt, which would lead to the same issue.

She sighed and bit the inside of her cheek.

'Is something wrong?' Connor asked.

'No, why?'

'I thought you sounded irritated.'

She smiled quickly. 'No, probably just a bit hungry. Walking must have built up my appetite. On the bridge you mentioned you've watched some Korean films. What other films do you enjoy?'

That was a safe topic, and he'd said he hoped she would get to know his tastes better as they spent time together.

After lunch they walked around the town.

'It's very beautiful here,' Connor said. 'This area is simply stunning.'

Rina gave a murmur of agreement, then breathed deeply, concentrating on staring ahead of her at the view she'd seen countless times before.

She sensed Connor staring at her.

He gently covered her hand. 'What's wrong?' he asked in a gentle tone.

She raised her eyebrows, surprised by his astuteness. 'It's hard to explain without sounding ungrateful and petulant,' she replied.

Connor smiled. 'It's okay to be ungrateful and petulant in front of me. I won't think less of you.'

The sincerity in his tone made her laugh. 'Okay, then,' she began. 'I grew up in England, but I barely remember living there. I moved to Switzerland when I was ten. Since then all I've seen is Switzerland—and even then not much of this country.'

He nodded his head in apparent understanding. 'You want to travel more.'

'Yes, but not only that. I want some adventure. I don't know how to explain it. I guess I just want a chance to live life to its fullest before I die,' she said.

He didn't say anything, only looked at her unblinking. It was refreshing to tell someone her deepest wishes. She didn't have any close friends to talk to, and her work colleagues all felt so lucky to be part of Lachance Boutique they couldn't understand her yearning to leave.

She waited for Connor to respond, unconsciously worrying at her bottom lip, hoping he wouldn't laugh at her comment.

'Apart from travelling, what do you want to do for adventure?'

She shrugged. 'I'm not a thrill-seeker, but I would like to try sky-diving or deep-sea diving. Perhaps learn the trapeze.'

Connor laughed. 'Why the trapeze?'

Rina grimaced. 'I know it's a bit random, but can you imagine flying through the air, relying on your own propulsion against gravity, nothing more than a net below?'

'Terrifying,' Connor said, shaking his head. 'I like having my feet on the ground. Although I have been deep-sea diving.'

'You have? Where? What was it like?'

'It was fun.'

Rina waited for him to say more, but Connor remained silent.

'You're so lucky, getting to visit so many places with work,' she said. She noticed him press his lips together. 'Don't you enjoy it?'

'It's a necessary evil. I travel more than I want to, and each time I get a promotion the travel increases. But I'm hoping soon I will be able to reduce the amount.'

Rina wanted to ask him more questions, but it felt too close to asking about his work and, arbitrary though it was, she was enjoying their hidden backgrounds.

'But you must enjoy travelling for leisure?' she said.

'Not particularly.'

Rina couldn't believe her ears. 'You don't?'

'I don't enjoy the feeling of living out of a suitcase.'

Rina couldn't help feeling there was something behind his statement—a reason he felt travelling for work was the same as living out of a suitcase. It sounded like a different kind of impermanence.

'Roots are important too,' she said.

'Very important.' After a moment's pause, he asked, 'Why did you move here?'

'Pardon?'

'You said you moved to Switzerland when you were ten. Why did you move?'

'Oh, that. I lost both my parents. They were killed instantly in a car crash.'

She tried to speak in a calm, dispassionate manner. So many years had passed; she believed she'd grieved fully for her parents, but recently she'd started to think about them and miss them. Perhaps it was the lack of inspiration in her work, perhaps it was the sameness of her existence but she couldn't help wondering what might have been if they had lived.

'I'm sorry,' he said.

He reached out and put a hand on her arm. He clearly meant it as a gesture of comfort, but her physical reaction to his touch was not comfortable in any way.

'It was a long time ago,' she said, moving away to get her heartbeat under control. 'Shall we carry on?'

She walked away without waiting for him to answer.

The next day Connor drummed his fingers on the steering wheel as he waited in his car. He was early. He wasn't due to meet Rina for another half-hour but he'd left himself plenty of time to get there. Because he didn't want to risk being delayed by traffic—not because he was in a hurry to see Rina. At least that's what he told himself.

He took out his phone, scrolling through new messages and emails that had come in during the hour since he'd previously checked.

There had been a flurry of activity in the team.

His meeting with Maria Lachance had been confirmed for the following day, which meant they were working on the final touches to his presentation. Usually he would curtail his leave to work on it too, but he knew his team didn't need him to micromanage them as long as he was contactable. And, with the meeting being tomorrow, this was the last day he would get to spend with Rina.

His heavy feeling at that thought was unusual and unexpected. Two words that described Rina, now he thought about it. She was different from the people he usually spent time with—open and free of artifice. Optimistic, with seemingly boundless energy, but not exhausting—which he often found was the case with people with similar personalities.

He wished he could spend more time with Rina, but that wasn't going to be possible. He felt there was so much to learn about her and she would be someone worth getting to know.

Perhaps he should arrange to stay in the area a little longer, in case there were issues to deal with after his meeting with Lachance Boutique.

He pinched his forehead. Was he really considering rearranging his entire schedule for the chance to spend a few more days with Rina? What was he hoping for from that? This wasn't the beginning of a relationship. He knew from experience that he was incapable of making the commitment necessary to sustain a lasting relationship. After a short while he always began to get restless and unsettled, ready to move on. Leaving was inevitable, as far as he was concerned. His childhood had instilled in him the idea of impermanence. Relationships were doomed because he was metaphorically packing his suitcase from the moment they began. He might be settled in one location for the most part, but that sense of intransience he'd grown up with hadn't changed, even though it was focused on a woman.

Once he left Switzerland he wouldn't try to keep in touch with Rina. There was no point. Work would inevitably get too busy and any contact would cease. It was better not to create any false expectations on Rina's part. They'd indulged in a brief flirtation, but it had never gone beyond that, they'd never give in to their attraction.

Perhaps it would be better if he cancelled today's plans with Rina—sent her a message to say that something had come up.

Even though he knew that would be for the best, he was still reluctant to take that step.

Five minutes later there was a knock on his window. He glanced up to see Rina, beaming at him. He took a sharp intake of breath. He now understood what it meant when someone had a smile that lit up their face and the day. At least the decision of whether to cancel their plans had been taken out of his hands.

He gestured for her to move away, then carefully opened his door.

'You're early,' she said, still grinning at him. 'I thought I'd be twiddling my thumbs, waiting for you, but you're already here.'

He nodded, unable to resist responding to her joyful expression with a grin of his own. He guided her round to the passenger side and opened the door for her.

It took them less than an hour to get to Mülenen, where they took the funicular to the summit of Mount Niesen.

Connor pointed at the staircase running beside them. 'Have you ever walked up those stairs?' he asked.

She shook her head. 'It's only open a few times a year. For some races.'

'You're not interested in taking part?'

'I would enjoy the challenge of doing the steps, but I'm not interested in the race.'

She scrunched her nose and he had to resist the urge to tap it...she looked so adorable. He forced himself to pay attention to what she was saying.

'I don't want to be part of a competition. Sometimes that takes all the fun out of it.'

'You don't think a little competition can make things more exciting?' he asked.

'Well, of course it can. For other people. I like watching competitive sports. I don't really want to be in them.'

So she wasn't competitive by nature. Connor automatically stored the information away with the other small nuggets she'd shared, helping him learn more about her. And the more he learned, the more he liked her. He had, by choice, always dated career-focused women—women who wouldn't ask much from him but who had a driving edge that occasionally made them come across as harsh. Rina wasn't like that. But he wasn't going to act on these nascent feelings when nothing could come of it. Particularly not when he was leaving Switzerland in a few days.

He closed his eyes briefly. Why was he even thinking about whether anything could come of this attraction he was certain was between them when they'd only met a few days before.

'Have you ever come here to watch the races?' he asked, in an attempt to keep their conversation prosaic.

'No. Perhaps I should. It's one of the few things to do around here.' Her smile was forced.

Connor could sense Rina's need to break out of whatever she felt was confining her. He might not share her desire to travel, but he could understand why she had such wanderlust. Perhaps if she had had his childhood, or had to travel so much for work, she would feel differently.

He immediately chastised himself. His childhood might not have been ideal, but his parents had chosen to take him and his siblings with them rather than dump them somewhere and travel alone—although they were doing that now. But even though he'd hated their nomadic existence, he couldn't imagine losing them when he was ten.

'It's a good job you're not afraid of heights, after all,' Rina said, bringing him back to an awareness of his surrounding and the motion of the train as it continued its ascent, as well as reminding him of the feeling of her body pressed close against his as they'd crossed the Sigriswil Bridge the previous day.

When they reached the summit, they spent some time gazing over the panoramic vista of Lake Thun. Even though they'd had an incredible view of the lake from the bridge, there was something about seeing it from this new height that made it more magical. Without fully understanding why, Connor reached for Rina's hand, as if clasping it would ground him in an otherwise fantasy world.

He huffed. And now he was thinking about magic and fantasy worlds! Despite the scenery around them, life wasn't a fairy tale, he wasn't a prince, and he didn't think anybody would describe Rina as a princess in need of rescuing.

They were two strangers who'd met by coincidence and happened to get along. Perhaps it was because that was unusual for him that he was giving it more importance than it deserved.

After they'd finished at Mount Niesen, they drove to a nearby town to have an early lunch. Connor desperately wanted to ignore the vibrations from his phone, but with the meeting taking place the next day, he couldn't leave his team in the lurch—they would only be contacting him if it was urgent.

He got up to excuse himself, but Rina held a hand up to stop him.

'Why don't you make your calls here? I can take a walk along the main street. There are some stores here that I like to visit when I come. Send me a text when you're ready to head back. I can tell you're busy, so we shouldn't stay out too long.'

Connor watched Rina leave. She didn't

seem upset that they wouldn't be spending the rest of the day together as they had originally planned. Had she offered to show him around only out of politeness after all? Perhaps the attraction was one-sided—although he was certain from the way she kept stealing glances and looking at him from under her lashes she did find him attractive.

But any attraction between them was a moot point.

He forced himself to turn his attention to the various emails and calls he had to respond to. After twenty minutes it was clear he would need to return to his hotel and work, cutting his day with Rina even shorter.

He sent her a text message and she responded within seconds, telling him where he should meet her.

He found her laughing with a store owner, trying on some Swiss hats. She looked happy and carefree. Wistfully, he wished he could wrap up her joy and keep some with him as a good luck charm. Instead he would have to say goodbye to her.

If she was disappointed to hear that he had to head back to his hotel she didn't show it. In the car she kept their conversation on neutral topics, talking about the area, making him wonder whether she was also carefully avoiding any further personal confidences.

The silence between remarks gradually got longer, the closer they got to his hotel.

Although he offered to drive her back to her village she refused, telling him she had some errands to do in the area and needed to visit the library.

When he finally parked, neither of them moved. Instinctively he knew he should get out to open her door for her, but once he'd done that it would really mean goodbye. Unless…

'If you're still in the area in a couple of hours, would you like to meet for an early supper?' he asked.

'Supper?'

'Dinner,' he clarified.

'Oh, I know what it means. I just didn't realise people still used that word.' She giggled.

Unable to resist this time, he affectionately tapped her nose. 'Cheeky.' He paused, suddenly serious. 'Would you like to meet for dinner?'

She inhaled. He wished he could guess what was going through her mind.

'Would it be like a date?' she asked.

He stiffened. They had spent a lovely day together, and admittedly he had been more than a little flirtatious, but he didn't want to give her the wrong impression.

He shook his head. 'Not a date. Even if it wasn't out of the question because I'm not here for much longer, I don't have time or space for a relationship in my life. It's a simple request for companionship so I don't have to eat alone.'

She grinned, and he found himself disappointed that she seemed pleased with his response.

'I completely agree. I'm glad we're on the same page,' she said.

'So, dinner?'

She didn't reply straight away. He wasn't sure whether it was because he'd been a little more curt than he'd intended in his question.

Finally she nodded. 'Okay, then, that would be lovely. Text me when you're free and we can meet for a spot of "supper",' she said, using a fake posh accent for the last few words.

Rina was nervous again. She couldn't understand why having dinner with Connor felt different, more intimate. They'd eaten lunch together, and after the initial awkwardness of sitting opposite each other they'd been easygoing with each other.

Perhaps it was the dim lighting, making the

restaurant look romantic—not at all appropriate for not-a-date. They should have met at a cheerful café or diner instead.

Rina looked through the menu. All the dishes were expensive—more than she'd usually spend on a meal. If this was not a date then she should expect to pay for her dinner or split the cost.

'Choose whatever you want,' Connor said. 'This is my treat, as a thank-you for being my tour guide the last couple of days.'

'You've already thanked me by buying lunch while we were out,' Rina replied.

Had he noticed her concern over the prices, or was he being generous?

'I'm very grateful for having my own personal tour guide.'

She didn't mistake the emphasis Connor placed on the word *personal*.

'Do you think you might come back to the Lake Thun area?' Rina asked.

Connor pressed his lips together. 'I have no immediate plans. Not for another year, probably.'

Rina bent her head, staring at her cutlery. Whatever these last few days had been, it was clear Connor had no interest in extending their friendship. She didn't regret spending those days with him, getting to know him better. It had been a brief interlude in her otherwise repetitive life. In a few hours it would be over, so she had to make the most of this time.

While they made their choices and ordered their meal Rina tried to come up with a topic of conversation which would be interesting, but not lead them down an intimate path. Something neutral. It was incredibly difficult to think of something. They'd already talked about films, and what they did for entertainment, and bringing up what they did when they were free in the evenings wasn't something Rina wanted to think about.

Connor put his elbows on the table and rested his chin in his hands, staring at her intently. 'What do you think of this restaurant?' he asked. 'The guide says it's excellent. Have you eaten here before?'

Rina giggled. 'No, never. Obviously I've heard about its reputation, but I never had the chance to eat here before. Thank you for inviting me.'

'No, thank *you*. It's the perfect way to end my holiday...having dinner with such an enchanting companion.'

Rina swallowed. Connor was being flirtatious again. And she liked it!

Her imagination immediately went to the

end of the evening—seeing him standing next to her in the illumination of the streetlight as she waited for her bus to arrive, his head bending slowly towards her, his mouth getting closer…

'Bon appetit.'

She almost groaned when her thoughts were interrupted by the arrival of the waitress with their first course.

Connor's lips twitched. She narrowed her eyes. There was no way he could have worked out the direction of her thoughts, was there?

'Tell me about the best restaurants you've eaten at,' she said, finally finding a neutral topic.

'I'm not really a foodie,' he replied. 'A steak tastes much the same whatever country you're eating it in.'

'You stick to what you know?'

'It's easier in some ways when I'm travelling. I do experiment with different recipes when I'm at home, though.'

'You cook?' She raised her eyebrows.

'Why does that surprise you?'

Rina tilted her head. 'Actually, it doesn't. Of course you would cook. You are the perfect man after all.'

Now she was the one flagrantly flirting— was she going to bat her eyelashes at him next?

The corner of Connor's mouth lifted. 'Is that what makes me perfect? My culinary expertise?'

'That's not the only thing,' she said, her voice turning husky.

'What else?'

Rina bit her lip. 'Well, you're fairly easy on the eye too.'

Connor laughed as he sat back in his seat, thoroughly at ease. 'That's quite the compliment. Thank you.' He mimed tipping a hat at her. 'How else am I perfect?'

She couldn't help the broad smile spreading across her face. 'What makes you think there's anything else?'

'Because you haven't mentioned my wit or charm yet.' He spoke in a serious, matter-of-fact tone, but there was no hiding the humour causing a twinkle in his eyes.

She pressed her lips into a pout. 'Hmm… I'm not sure I noticed that.'

'Really?' He smirked. 'Maybe I need to try harder, then.'

She dipped her eyes, then looked up at him from beneath her lashes. 'Maybe you do…'

She noticed him gulp, but their eyes remained glued to each other.

She had no idea how long they'd been staring and no idea how long they would have

continued if they hadn't been interrupted by
the staff clearing their dishes and bringing
the next course.

Over the rest of the meal both she and
Connor kept to light conversation, with no
more meaningful glances. Rina tried to convince herself she was happy with the way the
evening had gone, but it didn't work. If this
was the last night they would have together
she didn't want a quick, polite goodbye. She
wasn't exactly sure what she did want, but it
was something more than that.

As they left the restaurant, Rina turned to
Connor to begin their farewell.

Connor spoke first. 'It's still early. Do you
fancy taking a walk towards the lake?'

A walk in the moonlight next to a handsome man sounded perfect to Rina. So perfect she could hardly form words, merely
nodding in response.

They walked close to each other. Occasionally their bodies would come into brief contact before one of them hastily moved away.
Was he finding their touches frustrating, even
as much as they heightened the tension in the
atmosphere?

Her heartbeat became more erratic when
Connor's arm brushed hers as he pointed

something out to her, then casually slid his hand down her arm to grab hold of her hand.

Connor felt the warmth of Rina's tiny hand enveloped in his. These were the last few moments they would spend with each other. Technically he was at Lake Thun until Monday, since Maria Lachance had asked his company to keep the day free, in case she had any follow-up questions. He could conceivably spend the weekend with Rina. But he'd already told her he was there for only two days. And in the long run what would a few extra days matter? There was no chance of a relationship between them.

Rina had made it clear she would never leave Switzerland, and he couldn't imagine trying a long-distance relationship where he was constantly travelling to and fro—it would bring back too many memories of his nomadic childhood.

And something told him that if he spent extra time with Rina he would crave even more. It was best to say their goodbyes that evening, as planned.

'I should head to the bus stop now,' Rina said.

There was unmistakeable regret in her tone.

'Let me drive you home,' he offered. 'I

don't like the idea of you taking public transport alone so late.'

He would never get tired of hearing the crystal tones of her laugh. 'I'll be perfectly safe. Even my aunt doesn't worry about me travelling back on my own from here.'

'Please,' he pleaded.

He fully accepted that his offer wasn't purely out of concern for her safety—he wanted to prolong their time together, and he couldn't deny being in the close confines of his car with her was alluring. Maybe it was the fact that their brief time together was ending before he was ready to move on that was making it more difficult than he'd anticipated.

They spoke little on the journey back to Rina's village. He pulled the car to a stop in the lane near her home and got out, going round to open her door for her.

They stood next to the car, staring intently at each other; neither of them speaking. What was there to say? That he had a good time? That he enjoyed her company? That he wished he could be there longer?

All those things were true, but so true they didn't need to be said.

Unable to resist one final touch, Connor reached out and ran his fingers over her hairline, down over the nape of her neck and brought her braid to the front. Such glorious hair. Such a glorious woman.

He didn't know whether he moved first or Rina did; it was likely they moved in perfect synchronicity. But their arms went round each other, drawing them closer together, as his mouth covered hers hungrily. He groaned as she returned the pressure, demanding more, which he happily gave her.

CHAPTER FOUR

THE FOLLOWING DAY Rina was back working in her laboratory. The feelings of dull routine which she'd managed to dispel while she was spending time with Connor were now back in full force.

But she was trying not to think about Connor. And she was trying even harder not to think about their kiss. She didn't have the words to describe how amazing it had felt being in Connor's arms, exploring each other.

Rina watched as the vapour she'd extracted from the rampion began to condense in the flask to form the quintessence of Essence. Even the excitement she'd felt when she first cracked the extraction didn't hold a candle to the sensations that had wrought havoc in every fibre of her as she'd eagerly, greedily kissed Connor.

The only downside was the realisation it had been a kiss to say goodbye when it should have been a kiss to signal the start of something special.

What was he doing now? He'd told her he was travelling to Munich on business after his stay at Lake Thun. Was he on his way already? She wished she had a reason to leave with him. She wanted to visit Germany as much as she wanted to spend time with Connor.

Although she could empathise with Connor not enjoying all the business travel—it sounded as if it took some of the joy out of travelling—she had never been out of the country. She would love to leave Switzerland and see a little more of the world. But the chances of her aunt agreeing to that were slim. Rina had suggested they go abroad for vacations in the past, but Aunt Maria wouldn't leave—the idea was enough to cause her panic attacks to start. Any time Rina even raised the possibility of her going on her own she could see her aunt begin to tense and Rina hadn't the heart to pursue it.

She sighed and turned back to her flask, checking to see whether there had been any problems in the distillation process. But of course there hadn't. She would never want something bad to happen with her work, but

sometimes she wanted something different—
anything different—to happen.

She wanted to experience the joy she'd
felt when she'd extracted the exact proper-
ties she'd needed from the rampion to make
Essence work perfectly. But inspiration had
been missing for ages.

She watched as the gases condensed in the
cooler flask and the liquid dripped slowly into
the end container. She could almost feel her
own life energy dripping slowly away in the
same manner.

Her self-pitying thoughts were interrupted
a few minutes later by her aunt's personal assistant.

'Rina, Maria has asked you to go to the
conference room. The representative from
Newmans is about to give his presentation.'

Rina recalled her aunt moaning over breakfast that morning about having to meet with
someone from Newmans—yet another company that wanted Lachance Boutique, or at
least Essence by Lachance. Rina didn't blame
Aunt Maria for refusing all the offers they'd
received so far. None of them had seemed to
understand the ethos of Lachance. Many saw
money signs rather than an underlying need
to help people. There had even been companies that hadn't understood the importance

hair could have to some people. Still, Rina remained hopeful that a company would help her realise her vision of seeing Essence available more widely—probably unlike her aunt, who was comfortable maintaining the scale they currently produced—all part and parcel of her reluctance to deal with change.

It had become obvious from the consistent attempts at persuasion by companies they'd previously turned down that it was easier to meet representatives from these companies face to face, so she and her aunt could clearly outline their objections and reasons for refusal. They'd found they tended to take no for an answer in person rather than by email. Her aunt was a force to be reckoned with. It was hard to win any argument against her. Rina knew that for a fact.

Shaking her head to clear her thoughts, Rina took off her lab coat, checked her hair was mostly still in its bun, and then walked to the conference room. It was an impressive name for what was basically a small room with a dining table, but they made the best use of the space inside their tower, and she always believed the cramped dimensions added to the family atmosphere during staff meetings.

Rina knocked on the wooden door quickly,

then poked her head inside. Her aunt was seated at the head of the table. She gestured for her to enter.

'This is our head of product development, Katrina Lachance. Rina, this is Mr Portland from Newmans.'

Rina froze. The last person she'd expected to see again, and the one person she wanted to see again the most, was making his way towards her. When she thought about seeing Connor again it had never been in their own conference room. Was it her imagination, or had the room become smaller with Connor taking up almost all the space?

She was unsure how to react to seeing him again. She didn't want to face questions if she confessed they knew each other. Luckily, she was able to follow Connor's lead when he held out his hand.

'Pleased to meet you, Miss Lachance.'

'And you, Mr Portland.'

'Why don't you begin now,' her aunt ordered.

Rina tried to concentrate on Connor's presentation, which he was giving in fluent German. Why had he hidden his language skills from her? It made no sense. He had let her do all the talking when they'd visited places and in restaurants, even let her translate. Or had she assumed he couldn't speak the language and taken it upon herself to take over?

Why had he hidden the reason he was really in the area from her? He'd given her the impression he was taking a few days' holiday, not waiting for a business meeting.

Slowly she began to replay their meetings and interactions. Had it even been a coincidence when they'd first met in the fields near the tower? Had Connor always known who she was—the niece of the woman who ran Lachance Boutique and the developer of the coveted Essence. Was that the reason he'd been happy to spend time with her? Otherwise, why the secrecy?

What else had he hidden from her? There was probably a lot about him she didn't know. Even though she'd felt closer to him in a few days than she had to anyone before, she really didn't know him that well at all.

Hopefully the heat rising in her cheeks wasn't visible on her face; a combination of anger and humiliation that she, who prided herself on being a good judge of character, had been so taken in by him.

He wasn't going to get away with it—she would find a way to speak her mind to him. But for now she had to concentrate on business.

Slowly what Connor was saying began to

penetrate. She sat upright, paying closer attention. Finally someone had come up with a proposal that fitted almost exactly with how she envisaged the future for Essence and even Lachance Boutique itself.

Rina glanced at Aunt Maria to see if she appeared at all interested. Her aunt's smile was difficult to interpret. Rina could only cross her fingers and hope that her aunt would give them a chance to discuss the proposal together rather than reject it outright to Connor's face, as she often had in the past.

Rina felt slightly encouraged that her aunt might be feeling positive about the proposal when she listened to the questions her aunt asked. Usually Aunt Maria's questions were all to do with the reasons she had for objecting to the proposal, phrased in such a way that they could be interpreted as pressure-testing its strengths. Good company representatives could work out by that stage that they weren't going into business with Lachance Boutique.

She rolled her eyes at the idea of how good a company representative Connor was. All the charm, all that attention. Wining and dining her to get a business deal. She was almost tempted to turn Connor down, because she didn't want to be in business with someone who had deceived her. But she would be spitting in her own face if she acted rashly. Newmans proposal was simply excellent—too good to reject because of her personal feelings for their representative.

'Rina, do you have any questions for Mr Portland?' Aunt Maria asked.

'I have a few,' Rina replied. 'Is it okay for me to ask in German, or would you rather I spoke in English?'

Connor cleared his throat, and she didn't miss the faintest lift to his lips. 'Either is fine, Miss Lachance.'

She nodded, then went through the questions she'd noted during his presentation. He was able to answer confidently and fluidly.

Once the question-and-answer session ended, Connor began to pack his things away. Rina tried to come up with a reason to ask Connor to stay behind—she wanted, in fact needed, to give him a piece of her mind.

'Mr Portland, would you like a short tour of the place?' Aunt Maria asked, taking Rina by complete surprise. 'Not only is it our business premises, but it has interesting architecture as well. I'm sure you've observed our tower? It creates a lot of interest in this area.'

When Connor accepted, her aunt turned to her.

'Rina, I have a call to make. Please would you show Mr Portland round?'

'Of course, Aunt Maria.' She raised her eyebrows but her aunt's face remained impassive. Her aunt had never offered a tour to anyone from another company. Could this mean she was actually thinking about accepting Connor's proposal?

Rina banked down her excitement and concentrated on the prospect of confronting Connor. She had to know the truth—she had to know whether he had always known who she was. She had to keep a clear head. Right now, she had to think of Connor as the representative of a potential business venture—not the charming man she'd spent the last two days with. And she wasn't Rina Lahiri, pretend tour guide, but Katrina Lachance, head of product development and part-owner of Lachance Boutique.

'This is my laboratory,' she said, when they reached the closed sliding glass doors at the end of the tour.

Her aunt's assistant, Agatha, had accompanied them on the tour, which had made any private conversation difficult—for which Rina was grateful. There were too many questions that she had, none of which were appropriate for a business setting, the most pressing one being, had he known who she was? Was that the reason he'd wanted to spend time with her?

'How many people work in your lab?' Connor asked.

'Three, including me.'

'Only three? And you make all the products yourself, here?'

'We make the products. But we outsource packaging and distribution.'

'There would be huge potential savings on economy of scale if you accepted our proposal.'

'The decision on whether to accept your proposal will be solely down to Ms Lachance,' Rina said, wanting to make that clear to him.

She watched him closely for signs that the information affected him, in case he had got to know her because he thought *she* was the decision-maker, but she couldn't perceive any surprise or any other reaction from him. Was he a good actor or had he really not know who she was?

'I appreciate that, Miss Lachance.'

Did he place particular emphasis on her surname? This time it was Rina who cleared her throat as heat rose in her cheeks again. At least Connor hadn't lied about his name.

'I'm afraid I can't show you around the lab,' she continued. 'Proprietary products. I'm sure you understand.'

'Of course. But can you tell me how it feels, working in a circular room?'

Rina raised her eyebrows at the unexpected question. 'I feel like a magician in my tower. It's magical.'

Connor's lips quirked. 'I see. So there aren't any particular challenges posed by the shape of the room?'

Rina closed her eyes, wishing the ground would swallow her. She looked over at Agatha, who was covering her mouth with a book. It was bad enough to say something silly in front of Connor, without a colleague witnessing her embarrassment.

'Not at all,' she replied, deciding to embrace her comment. 'As I said, it's magical working here.'

Connor's mouth curved as he gave her an almost imperceptible wink. She couldn't help giggling at his charm, reminding her of the man she'd spent the last few days with and the man she'd kissed so passionately. Her giggles stopped abruptly as she caught Agatha's look of astonishment. This wasn't the same man. This was Connor Portland, businessman and representative of Newmans, who probably had more interest in Essence than in her.

'I shall leave you here, Mr Portland,' she said, putting out her hand. 'For now.' The look she gave him made it clear there was unfinished business between them and she *would* be seeing him later. 'Agatha will show you out.'

She wasn't sure whether their hands had remained clasped much longer than necessary because she hadn't wanted to let go, or because he hadn't. When he finally released her hand she twisted it inside her clothes, as if that way she could preserve the warmth and sparks of electricity that flowed through her.

'Connor.'

Connor turned when he heard Rina's voice behind him. He hadn't gone back to his hotel after his presentation. Instead he had come to the place they had first met, hoping she would somehow know to meet him there. And here she was.

He lifted his arms subconsciously, then forced them down by his sides. What was he doing—did he expect her to run into his embrace?

He remembered the lightness in his chest when he'd seen her walk into the conference room. Intense pleasure at seeing her again so unexpectedly, followed by shock at the realisation of who she really was and how important she was to his company. It had taken a tremendous effort to hide both reactions, but he'd worked out quickly, just by her posture, that she wasn't comfortable letting the people in the room know they already knew each other.

When she had told him she helped out her aunt, he had assumed she was referring to the older lady she'd been standing next to that first evening he saw her. He had never imagined she would be related to the owner of the company. And not only that. She was the creator of Essence, the miracle hair product. She was a genius. Somehow she had discovered a way to use the rampion that grew so abundantly around here in a hair product with the most amazing results.

He shook his head slowly, marvelling at the stunning, incredible woman in front of him.

She was glaring at him.

'What's wrong?' he asked, furrowing his brow.

'You're really asking me that? As if you don't know.'

He shook his head; he didn't know. If anything, he was the one who should be angry she had lied about her real name. But he wasn't. From what she'd shared about her aunt, it was a protective measure, and Lachance wasn't exactly a common surname. In this area it would be a complete giveaway about where she worked and lived.

'You seem annoyed with me,' he said, trying to keep a level tone.

'That's an understatement. Why didn't you tell me who you are?'

He blinked, bewildered by her question. 'I did tell you who I was, Rina Lahiri—or should I say Katrina Lachance.'

Her mouth twisted. 'Are you angry that I didn't tell me my real name?'

He smiled. 'No, I can understand that. I guess it was part of the reason you didn't talk about your job.'

'That was convenient for you, wasn't it?'

He furrowed his brow, perplexed. 'I'm sorry… I don't understand why it would be?'

'Because otherwise you would have had to admit why you really spoke to me that day.'

'You're the one who approached me,' he pointed out.

'Because I thought you might be lost. But that could have been part of your set-up.'

'Set up?' What was she talking about. 'I didn't know who you were, but perhaps I

should have guessed you worked for Lachance. You have such beautiful luxuriant
hair. I might have assumed you used their
products. I didn't know you'd developed
them.' He looked around him. 'I already told
you... I saw you in town my first evening
here. I thought you lived opposite the restaurant. You never contradicted me.'

'So you didn't approach me because you
knew I was part of Lachance Boutique and
thought spending time with me could help
you?'

His eyes widened as the reason for her attitude and questions finally dawned on him.
She suspected he had agreed to go sightseeing with her with ulterior motives.

'No, I admit I was there because I wanted
to see Lachance tower, but I never thought
about the business when I was with you.'

And that truth was alarming to his usual
work-driven self.

She bit her lip. 'So you really didn't know
who I was?'

'I really didn't.'

He smiled with relief when she nodded,
apparently accepting his response. He almost
reached for her again, but a glimpse of Lachance tower was a visual symbol of the al-
tered relationship between them.

'But now you know who I am. And I know who you are.'

'Does it make a difference?' she asked.

'Does what make a difference?'

'That we know now. Does it matter that I'm the product developer for Lachance and you're Director of the European Division for Newmans. Why can't we still be Rina and Connor?'

'We *are* still Rina and Connor,' he said emphatically, but then paused for a moment. 'But it does make a difference.'

She sighed. 'It does?' she asked somewhat ruefully.

'Mmm.'

'Why does it have to?'

'It makes a difference because now there's a business relationship between us.'

'A potential one.'

He quirked a brow. 'Until your aunt makes a decision on our proposal there's a business relationship between us.'

'And what was there before?' she asked.

'What?'

'Before today? What was there between us? Are we friends or was I just a tourist guide to you? A tourist guide that you happened to kiss.'

He grimaced. It was a simple question with

a complicated answer. What *were* they? He knew he liked her. He enjoyed her company. They were definitely on their way to being friends. But he was also attracted to her—a little too much for his peace of mind. For that reason alone, even trying to cultivate a friendship was probably a bad idea.

The business aspect was almost a minor additional factor.

'I don't know,' he replied eventually. 'Can people really become friends in only a few days?'

'What does the number of days matter when you feel a connection to someone? Friendships can be instantaneous.'

His eyes had widened at her use of *connection*. So she'd felt one too. Spending time with Rina was making him feel out of sorts, act out of character. He had to be sensible. There was no future for them. There couldn't be. He wasn't capable of offering commitment even to someone who lived in the same town as he did. Trying to make something work long distance would be impossible for him, and Rina deserved more than a brief affair. She was different from the kind of women he usually had affairs with—special in an indescribable way. Having a physical relationship with her would be wonderful, but he knew emotions would develop—hers, perhaps his—and that would be too messy for him.

He steeled himself not to react to her wistful expression. 'I have enjoyed your company,' he began, 'but I'm leaving for Munich soon, and then I'll be heading to India.'

'India?' her eyes widened.

'Yes, we have facilities in Mysuru and Bengaluru.'

The way her eyes brightened and lit up her face made him catch his breath.

'You're going to Mysuru?' she asked.

'Yes.'

'My mother grew up in Mysuru. I've always wanted to go but I never got the chance.'

'It's very beautiful there. I hope you get the chance to visit one day.'

He could almost see her brain ticking away. He didn't have to wait long to find out what she was thinking.

'Let me go with you,' she said, grabbing hold of his arm.

'What?'

He glanced pointedly at her hand, but she didn't remove it. Thankfully he was still wearing a jacket. If the sensation of the warmth and weight of her hand through its fabric was enough to evoke such a strong reaction in his body, he dreaded to think how he would have reacted if she'd rested her hand on his bare arm.

'Please. Let me go with you. I could come with you to Munich and then we could go to India together.'

A myriad of thoughts crossed his mind— the most startling of which was his urge to say yes. For that reason alone he had to say no.

'Rina, be serious.'

'I *am* being serious, Connor. Why can't I go with you?'

'You're being impulsive. You need to calm down and be sensible.'

He didn't mistake the hurt in her eyes, but she recovered quickly.

'Connor, I have always wanted to go to Mysuru. And you're going to Mysuru. Doesn't that sound like fate to you?'

'I don't believe in fate. It's a coincidence.'

She tutted, then sighed deeply, as if she was being extremely patient with him. 'Coincidence is just the cynic's name for fate. Anyway, you still haven't given me an actual reason why I can't come with you.'

Connor didn't think he'd ever met such a stubborn person. He didn't know what to make of it. He hoped she didn't want to go because she was hoping for a relationship with him. He had to make it clear to her that was impossible.

'I'm going for business, not for pleasure, Rina. I simply won't have time to entertain you.'

Rina tilted her head. 'I don't need you to entertain me. I can sort out a guide at the hotel.'

'What hotel? There are logistics to consider before travelling.'

'I'm sure I could get a flight at this time of year.'

'What about a visa? You'll need one for India. Those can take time.'

Rina shook her head. 'No, my mum sorted that out for me when I was a child. I have a card that means I can travel to India at any time. She always planned for us to visit every couple of years. And I'm sure I can sort out a hotel online. I can organise everything if you let me know your flight details.'

'Then why don't you organise to travel on your own or with your aunt another time? When you can plan it properly.'

'Because that will never happen.' Rina wrung her hands. 'I've wanted to travel so many times, but my aunt hasn't wanted me to. She worries about me, so I usually feel too guilty to pursue it.'

'What makes you think this time will be different?'

Rina practically deflated in front of him. 'I don't know if it will. But I know it never mattered so much to me before that I have to seize the opportunity. I just know that it's probably now or never for me. This could be my only chance.'

Connor paused. He wished he could help her, but it made no sense for her to travel with him. He was going to India for work—he couldn't take his girlfriend with him.

And Rina wasn't his girlfriend. He didn't know how to define whatever it was between them. They'd made a strong connection from almost the moment they'd met, but he knew it wouldn't last. He would never feel comfortable making a commitment to a girlfriend—he was too used to moving on. And even if a commitment was possible for him, Rina longed to travel…longed to explore. He travelled out of necessity—he would only clip her wings.

He shook his head. 'Rina, I—'

She placed a finger against his lips.

'Please, Connor, don't say no. Not yet. Think about it. Please.'

He felt the lingering warmth of her finger. He resisted the urge to run his tongue where her finger had been. Another sign that spending more time with her wouldn't be wise.

He didn't want to disappoint her, but there was no point giving her false hope that she could come with him.

'It's not a good idea, Rina,' he said, adopting a tone of finality.

Her shoulders slumped and she bent her head. He hated to see her that way, so different from her usually bubbly personality. But what could he do? He had to turn her down.

He reached out to touch her shoulder. Her head lifted at his touch. He stared at her, unable to hide the regret in his eyes.

Finally she grimaced, then asked, 'Will I see you before you leave?'

'I hope so. I'm going to be busy dealing with some of the points you and your aunt raised today, but I'll make time to say goodbye.'

'Okay. I'll see you then.'

She gave him a small wave before walking away.

He was sure he heard her mutter under her breath, 'Yeah, we'll see if it's goodbye.'

He barked a laugh. He should have known she wouldn't give up that easily.

CHAPTER FIVE

THE NEXT DAY Rina sat on her stool, watching and waiting for the extraction process to finish, the same as she'd done many times before. It might be a weekend, but that didn't mean much to her when her days all rolled into each other.

She *had* to find a way to convince Connor to take her with him. He was travelling to Mysuru. Connor might not believe in fate, but for her it was a clear sign that this was her chance to travel to India and visit the place her mother had lived as a child. Perhaps her only chance.

But even if she managed to convince Connor, she still had to convince Aunt Maria. She expelled a breath. One step at a time, though. She'd concentrate on Connor—that was her first hurdle.

There had to be something she could use to persuade him. She hardly had any time to come up with a compelling reason to tag along if she was going to get all the logistics sorted. She pulled out a notebook, ready to compile a list of ideas, but had barely managed to write a title before the intercom buzzed.

'Rina, do you have a moment to come here?' Aunt Maria asked.

'Sure.' She made sure her work was safe on its own, then went into her aunt's office.

'We didn't get a chance to speak properly about yesterday's presentation,' Aunt Maria said once Rina had sat down.

'It was good,' Rina said, pleased she could be truthful. She tried not to sound too enthusiastic—she didn't want to raise Aunt Maria's suspicions.

'I do feel it's the best one we've seen so far. And Mr Portland is very impressive.'

Rina nodded. 'But...?'

'I'm still not sure. It's good that the company's happy to start with a licence for Essence and doesn't want to take over Lachance.'

'That's true. So what aren't you sure about?'

'Do we really need it? Aren't we doing fine as we are?'

Rina sighed. This was the nub of the problem between their differing visions for Lachance Boutique. Aunt Maria was happy with maintaining the status quo, while Rina was of the firm belief if they didn't grow and improve they would stagnate. Someday, some company would be able to replicate Essence's formula and method, and then Lachance would have no chance to compete. If Rina couldn't come up with a new product what would happen to Lachance then? And since she'd been feeling wholly uninspired recently, she didn't hold out much hope for developing something new any time soon.

'Is "fine" enough?' Rina asked.

'It has been for many years.'

Lachance Boutique had been created by Rina's grandparents. Her aunt had joined the company, but Rina's dad hadn't followed in their footsteps since he'd moved to England after he'd got married. Aunt Maria was right that the company had done well for years, but it sometimes seemed to Rina that her aunt had forgotten they had almost been on the verge of changing direction or even closing before Rina had created Essence.

'But if we could get Essence into more hands… Wouldn't it be wonderful to think of people in more countries, even on different continents, using our product? But it's not something we can do on our own.'

Aunt Maria stiffened and pressed her lips

together. Rina hoped she hadn't gone too far. She knew from years of experience her aunt could be extremely stubborn once she'd made up her mind.

'I know that's what you want,' her aunt said. 'But is it really necessary?'

'We both agree that Essence shouldn't be a luxury product. But at the moment we can't sell it any cheaper. That keeps it out of a lot of people's price range.'

Her aunt inclined her head. 'I agree it's not ideal.'

'If we give Newmans a licence then we would have…' Rina tried to remember what Connor had said. 'We would have economies of scale.'

Aunt Maria smiled. 'It sounds like you actually paid attention to yesterday's meeting.'

Rina shrugged. 'It was the first time any of these business proposals chimed with me.'

'I agree that if we did go with any company it would be Newmans, but I still don't think it's necessary at the moment. Did you have any further discussion with Mr Portland when you gave him the tour?'

Rina willed herself not to blush, thinking about Connor and the way he'd looked when he'd grinned at her response to his question about the shape of her laboratory.

'Not really. He asked questions on how we were running the labs and our distribution. Then he said he was travelling to some of their other sites soon. They have a global enterprise.'

Her aunt tapped her chin. 'I would love to see how these companies actually work—see how their employees actually feel about the company and how it's run.'

Rina tried to contain her excitement at Aunt Maria's words.

'Why don't we?' she asked.

'What do you mean?'

'Why don't we go with Mr Portland and inspect his sites?'

'We can't just go like that. That's not how things work. Everything needs to be properly organised. We could maybe arrange a visit later in the year.'

Rina knew if they didn't take the opportunity now her aunt would never go.

'But wouldn't it be better if we went before they had time to plan anything. If we do this as an impromptu visit, we can see the facilities as they really are,' Rina said, sitting forward as her excitement built. 'Otherwise they'd put on a show for us, which would defeat the purpose.'

'Possibly.'

Rina held her breath, crossing her fingers that her aunt would agree.

'But,' her aunt continued, 'there's no point unless we are serious about their proposal. I have to admit Newmans impressed me more than any other company we've met with. But I'm still not convinced this is the right direction for Lachance Boutique.'

Rina sat back, deflated.

Her aunt turned back to the papers on her desk which was her way of indicating the conversation was over.

'I'll see you for dinner,' Rina said as she rose from her seat and left the room.

She made her way to the kitchen. She wasn't particularly hungry or thirsty, but since food and drink weren't allowed in the lab having a break would give her a few more minutes to gather her thoughts.

Her aunt's suggestion of seeing how the company really operated was excellent. So excellent, in fact, it was the perfect excuse for her to go with Connor. She clapped her hands as she expanded on the idea in her mind. He wouldn't say no if he believed Lachance might accept his company's proposal. And if the facilities were good Rina would definitely use all her persuasive powers to convince her aunt to seriously consider Connor's proposal. She would finally get the chance to travel—her dream come true.

Rina took a few centring breaths. She needed to be sensible. Her honesty compelled her to admit that the business advantage was secondary to getting to travel with Connor. But she had to determine how much of her excitement was to do with the prospect of travelling and how much was to do with the prospect of spending more time with Connor?

She liked Connor—enjoyed his company, found him attractive. *Very* attractive. She giggled again when the image of his gorgeous face appeared in her mind. But she wasn't naïve or foolish. She knew that there was no future with him. As much as she wanted adventure and excitement, Rina knew her duty was to remain with Aunt Maria. She owed her aunt too much to leave for a long time.

And Connor hadn't given her any indication he was interested in more than friendship from her. He'd even questioned whether their friendship was real. She shrivelled a little at the memory of how much that had hurt her.

But visiting Mysuru— something she'd wanted to do her whole life. Her aunt would never take her, Rina didn't have any close friends she could travel with, and she didn't want to travel on her own. If she waited for a time when her aunt felt happy to let her travel she could be waiting all her life. And getting to visit the birthplace of her mother was worth pushing the idea with Aunt Maria. She might never get this chance again.

She had no concerns about travelling with Connor—she trusted him. She'd already spent enough time in his company to know that he was a decent man with integrity. She had to seize this opportunity with both hands.

Without hesitation, she took out her phone to send Connor a message, asking him to meet with her as soon as he was free, offering to go to his hotel if it was easier. She sighed with relief when he agreed to come to their field in an hour.

The time it took before she saw Connor approach her in the field felt like the longest time of her life. She would still need to tell her aunt of her decision, but her priority was to convince Connor. And the best way to do that was to make it part of a business proposal.

She gave another quick look over the file she had prepared before she'd come to meet Connor. It outlined the rationale for her to accompany him on his visit. Although he already knew she had personal reasons for wanting to go to Mysuru, she was pleased her business rationale was solid in itself.

He had to say yes.

She had fully expected him to refuse when she'd first mentioned her proposal, but it had still been disappointing to see his immediate negative reaction. He clearly wasn't interested in spending more time with her now that he'd mentally compartmentalised her as a business contact—so it was a good job she wasn't after any kind of relationship with Connor. She just wanted a travel companion, someone her aunt would consider trustworthy. She needed to stack the deck in her favour when she spoke to her about her plans. She was adamant she would be travelling with Connor.

She handed him the file. 'Read through this. It explains everything better than I did.'

She watched Connor closely as he looked through her file. He frowned once he'd finished.

'Do you mean that unless I take you with me, you won't be prepared to consider our offer?' he asked.

Rina furrowed her brow. It sounded as if she was extorting him when he put it that way.

'No,' she replied forcefully. 'Lachance Boutique would still do their…um…due diligence before accepting any proposal. Newmans' proposal happens to be the one we're most interested in at present.'

'There's no guarantee your aunt will accept our offer even after your visit.'

'No, there isn't,' she admitted, and then played the ace in her hand. 'But she listens to me, and my views carry a lot of weight.'

'What is it you're trying to say?'

'I don't understand all the legal stuff myself, but I'm part-owner of Lachance Boutique.'

'What does that mean for Newmans?'

'It means I can use my influence to convince my aunt to grant you a licence at a fair market value. I already know she's open to your business proposal, and I can sway her decision in your favour.'

'What makes you think you can persuade your aunt to give us a licence when you can't even persuade her to let you travel on your own?'

Rina's mouth gaped open. 'That's unfair. Aunt Maria doesn't want me to travel because of the accident. There is no correlation between that and me trying to persuade her to give you the licence.'

'What accident?'

'I told you my parents died in an accident. I was in it too.'

Connor inhaled sharply. 'You were in the accident?'

Rina nodded. 'We were on our way to the airport to collect Aunt Maria. She wanted us all to go on a trip straight after collecting her, otherwise I would have stayed home with my mum. I think she's always felt a bit guilty about that. That's why she gets panic attacks at the thought of travelling, and why she worries about me travelling.'

'Aren't you concerned about worrying her, then?'

Rina bent her head. Perhaps she was making the biggest mistake in her life, but her gut was telling her she had to go to Mysuru with Connor. She had to grab the opportunity of living out her dream, regardless of the consequences. Rina loved her aunt, and didn't want to deliberately hurt her. But she had to believe that Aunt Maria loved her too, and in the end her love would be strong enough to accept Rina's need to travel. Hopefully, once Rina returned unharmed it would help her aunt to worry less about her.

'Of course I am. But I have to do this.' Rina expelled a breath. 'Connor, I'm sure I'll be able to convince my aunt to accept your proposal. And, really, I'm the best—probably the only—chance you have of that.'

'You think she would turn us down otherwise?'

She nodded. 'Yes. So, will you take me?'

She held her breath.

CHAPTER SIX

CONNOR GLANCED OVER at Rina, sleeping peacefully in the passenger seat. Although he should be annoyed, he couldn't help smiling. He wasn't surprised that she'd got her own way and they were now driving together to Munich on his visit there before they flew to India.

His company had been more than happy to make arrangements to accommodate her when he'd told them Rina was interested in inspecting some of Newmans' sites to make sure the company was a good fit for Essence. They understood her interest to be a positive and encouraging sign, since no other company had received that. The board had indicated his promotion was pretty much in the bag but would only be announced once Lachance Boutique signed on the dotted line.

He pressed his lips together. This promotion had been his goal pretty much since he'd been promoted to his current position. And now it was in his grasp thanks to Rina.

He didn't flatter himself Rina wanted to travel with him for the pleasure of his company—India held the true allure for her. If he hadn't been travelling to Mysuru would she still have been interested in persuading her aunt to grant the licence for Essence to his company? He didn't usually doubt his skills and abilities, but if his promotion was dependent on finalising the deal with Lachance Boutique, he wanted to be absolutely certain he'd earned it.

Rina mumbled something in her sleep, then turned to her other side so she was facing away from him. Although she'd been bright when he'd collected her, she'd fallen asleep within half an hour. He'd expected her to be tired, since they'd set off quite early that morning. It would take around four hours to drive to Munich, and he wanted to arrive before eleven. But he was still disappointed not to be listening to her chatter away.

Rina's aunt hadn't come out to say *bon voyage*. He wondered whether that was because of their early start time or whether her aunt was unhappy with Rina's insistence on entertaining Newmans' proposal. Or was it something else? He grimaced. Hopefully Rina's desire to travel hadn't caused too much conflict with her aunt. But ultimately, as long as the deal went through, it was none of his business.

Whatever he and Rina had been to each other when she'd been showing him around Thun, now there was only a business relationship between them—and he would maintain a professional attitude. He had to take all personal talk off the table.

It was actually a good thing Rina was sleeping so he didn't have to indulge in any small talk.

After driving for a couple of hours, he pulled into a restaurant. He reached over to wake Rina. He said her name quietly, causing her to turn her head towards him. The shadows on her face emphasised her high cheekbones and her straight, dainty nose. There was no denying she was gorgeous. But he wasn't supposed to have those thoughts about her.

He gently shook her shoulder.

'Rina,' he said quietly. 'Rina, wake up. We've stopped to have some breakfast.'

She came awake with a jolt, automatically putting her hand up to wipe over and around her mouth. He grinned. He could reassure her that she hadn't drooled while she was asleep.

'We still have a few hours' drive. Time for a coffee. Come on.'

He got out of the car and walked round to hold her door open for her.

She took a couple of moments to orientate herself, then reached under the glove box to grab her bag.

As soon as she got out of the car she stretched and yawned, not bothering to cover her mouth. He couldn't help laughing as he watched her rub her eyes.

'What?' she asked, mid-rub.

'You remind me of a raccoon?'

'A raccoon? Has my make-up smudged?' she muttered, reaching into her bag, 'No, wait, I'm not wearing make-up. Did you say raccoon?' she asked, as if unsure she had the correct translation. 'The animal?'

He nodded, trying to hide his smile.

'You think I look like a raccoon?' She huffed.

'A very cute raccoon.'

She quirked an eyebrow.

'The cutest raccoon I've ever seen,' he added for good measure, pleased to hear her chuckle.

'You need to work on your compliments,' she said wryly.

'Being compared to a raccoon is possibly the highest praise I can give.'

'Hmm, sure.' She rolled her eyes.

He needed to stop the flirtatious banter, but it would take a while to adjust to their new solely business relationship.

They walked into the restaurant and were led to a table. After they'd ordered, he deliberately took out his phone and scrolled through messages and emails while they waited for their food.

Without batting an eyelid, Rina took a notebook out of her bag and started jotting down notes and making sketches. He found it hard to concentrate on his phone, curious to know what she was writing.

They both put the items away when the food came.

'Are you sure I can't drive part of the way?' Rina asked after they'd taken a few bites. 'I have a driving licence.'

'I'm fine. Anyway, it's a hire car and I didn't add you.'

'Okay. Stop as often as you need.'

'I plan on driving straight through now. Unless you're going to need bathroom breaks?'

Rina shrugged. 'Who knows? Are you going straight into a meeting once we get to Munich?'

'Pretty much—but it will depend on what time we finally arrive. Newmans has arranged for someone to show you round the office while I'm busy, then we'll both go to the distribution centre. After that we can check in to the hotel. I have a dinner meeting, which will probably last most of the night, so you'll have the evening to yourself.'

She nodded slowly. 'Sounds good. It's a shame we're too late for Oktoberfest. I would love to go to that. How weird that it mostly happens in September. Have you ever been?'

'No. I've been to Munich when it's on, but never had time to take part. I'm there for work.'

She pushed out her bottom lip. 'Seems a waste. But I suppose that's what happens with business travel. You've never wanted to go there for pleasure?'

'No.'

His abrupt response made it clear he didn't want to discuss the topic further. Why was that? Was there something he didn't want her to know? Some kind of secret he was hiding? Perhaps it was something personal to him and he didn't feel close enough to tell her yet—although that idea made her sad, she respected his privacy and wasn't going to press the issue.

They carried on eating for a few more minutes before Rina asked whether she'd be able to access the internet in his office.

'I want to send the notes I just made to my colleague,' she explained.

'I'm sure someone can arrange that for you,' Connor replied.

'Actually, that's okay. I don't know whether I can encrypt it properly.'

'Encrypt?'

Rina gave an embarrassed laugh and shrugged. 'I don't really know what I mean… It's not usually an issue, since we all work off the same system in the tower. But I had a great idea when I saw those dewberries outside and I want to share it as soon as I can. But I can almost hear my aunt warning me it could turn out to be a trade secret so I have to be careful. There's so much to think about when you travel for work…' She exhaled forcefully.

Connor blinked. 'You had an idea based on a plant you saw outside for a second?' He hadn't noticed any of the scenery.

'Yes, I recognised its fruit immediately and it occurred to me…' She trailed off. 'It's not important.' She turned to look out of the window. 'It's so picturesque. I'm going to try to stay awake for the rest of the drive.'

Connor didn't say anything. His company employed some excellent scientists, but he wondered whether any of them would come up with an idea worth sharing based on a brief glimpse of a flower or anything else. Of course he didn't know for sure whether Rina's idea had any merit, but he got the impression, from everything he'd heard about Lachance's product designer, that she was incredibly skilful and professional. He doubted she would share any idea with her colleagues unless it had real potential.

Rina was quiet in the car for the rest of the drive. She spent the time looking at the scenery and writing in her notebook, nodding often.

He wished he could ask more about what she was working on. But whereas before they had constructed an artificial barrier to take work off the table, now there was a real barrier preventing them from talking about work. She would probably assume any curiosity on his part was because of his company rather than out of a desire to understand more of her thought processes, because she, quite simply, intrigued him.

He had anticipated he would regret Rina accompanying him on these visits. So far everything was confirming his view.

* * *

Apart from a couple of occasions when he stopped to take some calls in private, they made good time to Munich.

'I have around forty-five minutes before my meeting,' Connor said. 'Why don't we find a café nearby and have a coffee?'

He would enjoy some more time with Rina before heading into the bustle of work.

'Can't we go to your office early?' Rina replied, surprising him.

'I'm sure we can. The person who's going to give you the tour may not be free, though.'

'That's fine. If you can find me somewhere to sit, and a desk, I'll be fine.'

He could tell her mind was elsewhere—possibly on the idea she'd had over breakfast.

This focus was an interesting aspect of her personality he might never have discovered if she hadn't joined him. If he'd based his opinion of her on the two days they'd spent together touring around Lake Thun he would have described her as someone who enjoyed life, looked for the fun in it and didn't take anything too seriously. Discovering she had created Essence had got him reassessing his initial opinion.

He wondered what else he would learn about her as they spent more time together.

Despite his determined efforts not to get closer to her, he was looking forward to discovering more facets of Rina.

Rina's first few hours in Munich had passed by in a whirl of activity. Initially the people she'd seen at the Newmans office and at its distribution facility were understandably curious about her presence, but once she'd been introduced and they heard her surname their attitudes changed.

Rina supposed it was gratifying that so many people knew about her product—particularly when they couldn't yet afford to advertise widely. Essence had become known through word of mouth and beauty influencers. Sometimes, stuck in her small lab in her small tower, she had no idea exactly how popular her products were on a human level—sales sheets and profit and loss accounts were a dry metric.

They'd finally checked into their hotel just after five p.m. After a wash, Rina sat on the bed in her room, looking through the room service menu. Connor had his business dinner so she would be eating alone.

She pursed her lips. This was the first time she had been outside Switzerland—she didn't want to spend the night cooped up inside, eating in her hotel room. Perhaps she could get a recommendation from Reception about a good place to eat that was easy to get to on foot.

If only Connor were free to go out with her. Not because she didn't want to eat alone, but because she enjoyed things more when she was with him. Although he had been strange with her that day—different from usual. She guessed he might still be annoyed that she'd managed to get him to take her with him—or maybe it was just all the driving he'd done.

She grimaced. She could understand why he didn't enjoy travelling for work so much if a hotel room was all he got to see of the places he went to. Perhaps if she had to travel for work she would also find it annoying. But she found that hard to believe. So far her time in Munich had been all about business, but she still thrived on the knowledge she was in a different country, even if in many respects it wasn't that different from her home.

And soon she'd be in India.

Although she'd convinced Connor about her business reasons for travelling with him, he knew her main reason was visiting her mother's homeland. Finally getting a chance to see the place her mother had grown up in, hoping to find a sense of connection with her that she'd missed growing up in Switzerland, where there was nothing to remind her of her mum.

She pulled out the photo she had in her purse. It showed her as a toddler in her mother's arms. Her father had his arms round both of them. It was her favourite family photograph and she always carried it with her.

Aunt Maria had done an incredible job of being a substitute parent figure; Rina had grown up wanting for nothing—it almost made her feel guilty for missing her parents. And now she was missing her aunt. They had never spent much time apart. Even when Rina had gone to university, Aunt Maria moved to the same city, so they could live together. And, although her aunt's overprotectiveness frustrated her on occasion, she understood how her aunt felt—losing nearly everyone she loved in one moment, and almost losing Rina too. Aunt Maria had patiently helped with her rehabilitation and raised her with no thought for herself. Rina owed her so much.

She tried calling her, but there was no answer. Her aunt's lack of response was threatening to dampen the joy of her travelling. She could understand why her aunt was unhappy, but she'd hoped her aunt would be able to understand why she *had* to travel to India. Perhaps Aunt Maria just needed time. She would still leave messages to let her aunt know she was safe.

In the end, she decided to go down and ask in Reception. The restaurant suggested by one of the receptionists was excellent. She ate a lovely meal and enjoyed chatting to the owners when they weren't busy with other diners. They insisted on someone escorting her back to her hotel.

When she went inside, Connor was pacing in the foyer.

'Where have you been?' he demanded, stalking up to her.

She frowned. Why did he sound angry and as if he'd been scared? 'I went out for dinner. Is something wrong?'

'I tried calling you and went to your room. There was no answer. I had no idea where you were.'

'I was at dinner,' she repeated, wondering why he was making such a fuss. 'I had my phone in my bag…on silent.' She pulled out her phone and noticed a number of missed calls. He couldn't have been that worried about her, could he? She'd been perfectly safe.

'Why didn't you tell me?' he demanded. 'Or leave me a message.'

She felt as if she was being scolded by the school principal.

'What's wrong with you, Connor? You told me you'd be busy all evening. I didn't think my whereabouts would concern you.'

'You're alone in a strange city—for the first time, I might add—and you didn't think I would care where you were?' There was no mistaking the incredulity in his tone.

She rolled her eyes. She already had an overprotective aunt; she didn't need an over-protective travel companion too.

'I may not have travelled much before, but I assure you I'm perfectly capable of navigating a new place on my own. I didn't take unnecessary risks. I wouldn't do that. I was perfectly safe. In fact, I met a lovely family. They own the restaurant I ate at and they've invited me back for lunch tomorrow. But I may try somewhere new. I don't know.' She pasted on a smile. 'Anyway, it's been a long day. I think I'll go up to my room.'

'This conversation isn't finished.'

Well, he would have to continue it with himself, because Rina was already summoning the lift.

He got in beside her, staring straight ahead. Their rooms were on different floors, but he made no move to exit when the lift passed his. Perhaps he had misunderstood her move towards the lifts as a suggestion that they should continue discussing the matter in her room, rather than a declaration that she wasn't listening to him anymore.

Accepting the inevitable, she exited the lift and walked to her room, aware that Connor was following her. She hoped she'd left the room in a suitable state for company, but she'd pulled things out of her case in a hurry. She couldn't guarantee there wasn't underwear on the floor.

She scratched her head. What were the chances Connor would agree to wait outside while she quickly picked things up? She glanced behind her. He was still looking grim. He wasn't going to let her out of his sight before he'd had his say.

The door had barely closed before Connor said, 'In future I would appreciate it if you would let me know where you're going.'

'Pardon?' Rina asked, raising her eyebrows.

'While you're travelling with me, I'm responsible for your safety. I would appreciate you letting me know your whereabouts.'

He spoke calmly. He almost sounded reasonable. But...

'You're not responsible for me, Connor. I'm an adult. I'm responsible for myself. I don't take unnecessary risks.'

'You don't think it was a risk going out alone in a country you've never been to before? At night? In the dark?'

'I went to a place that was recommended to me by someone at this hotel. They told me there would be lighting the whole way and it was barely more than five minutes' walk.' She spoke extra-slowly, enunciating every word. 'And one of the owners even walked me back to the hotel. I was perfectly safe.'

'You walked back with a stranger and you talk about not being reckless?' he scoffed.

Rina tightened her jaw. 'I got to know the family during dinner. By the time I'd finished he was less a stranger to me than you were when I offered to be your guide. That was probably more reckless than going out to dinner tonight,' she said.

Or was that the problem? Had her behaviour with him on their first meeting given him cause for concern?

Connor pinched the bridge of his nose. She could tell he was reaching the limits of his patience with her.

'Rina, I didn't know where you were. Anything could have happened. You were alone in a strange city. I was worried about you.'

Hearing the concern in his tone, all the antagonism left her.

'I'm sorry. I didn't think you'd notice my absence. I promise you don't have to worry about me. I'm not going to take risks with my safety. But you aren't responsible for me. Any more than you'd be responsible for another work colleague.' Rina's mouth fell open. 'Oh! You probably *do* think you're responsible for your colleagues when you travel.'

Connor turned away from her, confirming her suspicions. She didn't know why, perversely, knowing he would worry about anyone made her more annoyed. Had she hoped she was special to him in some way? That there was a personal concern for her?

She closed her eyes. It didn't matter how attractive he was, or how much she enjoyed his company, nothing could happen between them. No romance, a tentative friendship at most. She should be *pleased* she wasn't special to Connor, not disappointed.

'It's been a long day. I'm tired. I think I'll go to bed now, Connor.'

Heat rose in her cheeks. It was a bad idea to think of Connor and bed in the same sentence.

She turned her thoughts to more boring matters. 'Will you be going downstairs for breakfast?'

They agreed on a time to meet the next morning.

'Have you decided what you're going to do tomorrow?' he asked.

'Not yet,' she replied, walking to the door and holding it open. 'Once I do, I'll make sure to send you a detailed itinerary.'

Connor's jaw tightened. As he walked past her to leave, he paused and opened his mouth—then he must have changed his mind, because he simply nodded and left.

Rina expelled a breath as she let the door close. Dealing with Connor was as bad as dealing with her aunt.

That reminded her that she still hadn't had a chance to speak to Aunt Maria. There was still no answer when she called—it was beginning to look like her aunt was avoiding her.

Her aunt hadn't been pleased when Rina had told her she was going to travel with Connor. At first she'd tried to change her mind. Rina could easily recall the look of disappointment and unhappiness on her aunt's face when she'd refused to back down.

Rina felt she'd betrayed her only family.

She left a perky voicemail message, knowing her aunt would want to be reassured she

was all right, even if she was currently unhappy with Rina.

Rina walked over to the window. It was her
first time in a different country and she could
explore to her heart's content the following
day. But instead of feeling excitement or anticipation, she felt frustrated and stressed.

She could only hope a good night's sleep
would put her in a better frame of mind.

CHAPTER SEVEN

CONNOR'S GAZE KEPT going to Rina, who was standing by a large window, looking at the planes take off and land. She'd been jittery ever since they got to the airport.

He could understand she must be very excited to be travelling to India—something she'd wanted to do all her life—but he couldn't help feeling there was something underneath all that excitement.

He recalled her setting off the security scanner earlier. It had been due to a metal zip, but she'd joked to him afterwards that for a moment she'd worried that the implants she'd had as a child had set it off. He'd assumed she was referring to her injuries from the accident which had killed her parents.

He couldn't help admiring this woman, who could find the humour in such a situation. At the same time he wanted to take her in his arms and offer her comfort she hadn't asked for and probably didn't need.

She had such a positive outlook and cheery disposition—in some ways the complete opposite personality to his—it would be easy to believe there were no long-lasting effects from the devastating loss she'd suffered as a young child. But her determination to go to Mysuru with him showed clearly how much she must miss her mother.

In that respect, it was hard to stay annoyed with her for effectively bribing him to bring her along with him. He still should be. But she was completely unapologetic about what she'd done. As far as she was concerned, theirs was a mutually beneficial arrangement. And, seeing how excited she'd been when she'd heard he was going to Mysuru, and knowing how much visiting her mother's birthplace meant to her, he doubted he would ever have had the heart to turn her down.

He narrowed his eyes with concern as he continued to look at her. Although she was still smiling, there was a tension in her shoulders he'd never seen before.

He walked over to her. 'Everything all right?' he asked.

She looked up at him, her smile brightening, causing his breath to catch. 'Yes, it's surprisingly addictive watching all the planes,' she replied, pointing to one getting ready to taxi.

'You haven't had anything to eat or drink. Are sure you don't want something? It could be a while before we get any food on the plane.'

She patted her stomach, drawing his attention to its flatness and the trim waist beneath it. He forced himself to look away before he embarrassed himself by being caught admiring her figure.

'I don't think I could eat anything at the moment,' Rina replied. 'Maybe I'll grab some fruit.'

'Good idea. We should probably head down to the gate in fifteen minutes.'

She nodded, but was already turning back to the window.

When their flight was called he noticed Rina looking around her, taking in everything as they boarded the plane, soaking it all up.

'This is something special, isn't it?' she commented, looking around the business class cabin. 'I suppose it's more comfortable for you with the extra leg room.'

She stretched her legs out in front of her, wiggling them to show how much space she had.

She was probably shorter than average

for a woman, but since he was over six foot two, he never paid much attention to people's heights—they were all usually shorter than him. Although now he couldn't help imagining enfolding her in his arms and resting his chin on the top of her head, the memory came to him of how he had lowered his head as she'd reached up to him before their mouths met for their first kiss.

He cleared his throat, trying to remember what Rina had said. Something about her legs…no, leg room.

'I usually work on the flight, so additional room is helpful. Why don't you give the flight attendant your coat? Make yourself comfortable.'

He grinned a few moments later as he heard Rina's squeal as she inspected the contents of her amenity bag. She sounded the way as other people did when they received expensive gifts.

'What was that?' Rina asked, suddenly clutching his arm at a noise.

'The engines.' He furrowed his brow. 'Are you nervous about flying?'

'A little bit…'

His eyes widened with concern when he saw Rina's stiff, pale face. It suddenly dawned on him that if she hadn't travelled outside

Switzerland before, this would be her first time flying.

He reached across and gently took her hand in his, giving it a squeeze. 'Okay?' he asked.

She gave him a small, excited smile which couldn't quite hide her nerves. She leaned forward to try and catch a glimpse outside.

'I'm sorry,' Connor said. 'I should have thought to arrange a seat by the window for you.'

Rina cast a glance around the cabin. 'It's fine. All the window seats are singles. Sitting in the middle like this, I get to hold your hand.'

She closed her eyes and squeezed his hand tighter as they felt the plane begin to move.

'Would it make you feel better if I explain the physics behind how flight is possible?' he asked.

She laughed, as he'd hoped she would. 'That's okay, thanks. It's odd, feeling this excitement, but slight anxiety as well.'

'I understand. In less than twenty hours you're going to be in India. Have you made any plans for your free time?'

'Nothing specific yet. I have guidebooks in my cabin luggage. I'll look through them when we're in the air. I guess I haven't really thought further than getting to the country.

Of course I want to see my mum's old home, but that won't be until we get to Mysuru.'

'What do you know about Bengaluru and Mysuru already, then?' he asked, trying to keep her talking.

He managed to distract her with small talk until the plane had taken off and they were free to move around the cabin.

She released his hand. He almost tried to grab hers again, seeking its warmth and pressure.

'Why don't you try to get some sleep?' he suggested. 'We're at the beginning of a long journey.'

'I'm not going to sleep yet. That would be such a waste of my first experience on a plane. I'm going to choose a couple of movies…maybe try out the games.'

She laughed, the sound bright and joyful, as if her happiness and excitement had to bubble out of her.

She was completely absorbed during the flight, restful, enabling him to make good progress on his work. He noticed her tension return when the captain announced the plane was ready to land.

As soon as she'd returned her seat to the correct position, he reached over and took hold of her hand again.

'First leg of our journey almost over. How was it?' he asked.

'Wonderful. Truly wonderful. But I don't think flying business has given me the real experience of a long-haul flight. I'd like to know what it's like flying in the other class.'

By 'other class', Connor knew she didn't mean first. It was typical of the Rina he'd come to know that the only thing she'd said that might remotely be construed as a complaint was that she'd travelled in relative comfort.

He considered whether they could change one of the remaining legs of their journey to 'the other class'—he wanted to give her the chance to experience everything she wanted to.

If it was possible, he would also see whether they could have a day's layover in Doha on their return leg, or maybe add other stops to their trip.

Why was he spending time thinking about how he could help Rina have some more of the adventure she craved? They were business colleagues now. If there had ever been a possibility they could be something else before he'd known she was a Lachance, then it had been slim and in the past.

Getting the licence, and potentially his promotion, was too important to jeopardise with a brief flirtation. And that was all it could ever be. He wasn't good at making commitments to women, and he'd learnt from experience that it was better not to pretend it could happen. And Rina wasn't like his previous partners—in many ways she was still innocent.

How innocent was she? She spoke about how protective her aunt was, which must make having a boyfriend difficult.

He immediately shut off that train of thought. They'd already had their brief flirtation, when he hadn't known she was part of Lachance Boutique. They couldn't go back to that time, and there was nothing in the future for them but a business relationship.

By the time they were off the plane and resting in the airport lounge in Doha, Rina was back to her usual self. There were no signs that she was nervous about their flight to Bengaluru, but he managed to persuade her to have a massage treatment in the airport spa, to ease out any tension so she could relax fully before the final leg of their journey.

Rina was busy scribbling in her notebook for most of their layover. Her passion as she worked was evident. Connor pressed his lips together. He enjoyed his work, but it had been a long time since he'd felt that kind of passion for what he did. Hopefully, if he got the promotion, some of that would return.

When they were on board the next plane, there were still no signs of anxiety from Rina as they got ready for take-off. She was talking animatedly to some of the flight attendants while the passengers in the other cabin boarded.

Rina flipped through a magazine as the flight took off. He flexed his hand, as if it missed the chance of holding on to Rina's again.

She was a little more restless on this flight, fidgeting next to him. He could have ignored her and concentrated on his work. Instead he put his laptop and papers away and offered to play a game or watch a film with her.

She turned down his suggestions, telling him she was too excited to focus.

'Can I just ask you questions instead?' she asked.

'About work? Sure.' Connor suspected that was the only safe topic of conversation for them.

Rina pouted, showing that wasn't her original intention, but she asked, 'Does your company have offices in any other parts of India?'

'We do. I'm the director of European Operations so I don't usually visit the Indian offices, they're not in my remit but the director of South Asian operations, Nihal Murty, is new to the post. He used to work with me and I recommended him for the position, so I'm going out to discuss any issues he has as kind of a favour.'

If Connor received his promotion he would have many meetings, with directors of all the different sectors, but in future they would travel to him rather than the other way round.

'He knows I'm coming?' asked Rina.

'Yes. He's a trained scientist too, so he's looking forward to discussing your work.'

'Oh, I'm not trained as a scientist,' Rina said with a sombre expression. 'My aunt just knows I like playing with chemicals, so she lets me experiment with them. It seems to work.'

'Pardon?' Connor said, his eyebrows flying to his hairline.

Laughter pealed from Rina. 'If only you could see your face right now,' she managed to gasp out, pointing at him. 'Of *course* I'm trained! In fact I was offered the chance to do a PhD, but I went into the family business instead.'

Connor sighed, as if pained by her joke. If only she could see how stunning her face was when she laughed. Breathtaking. Adorable. He didn't know the right description for her beauty.

He looked away quickly. Maintaining a businesslike, professional distance was becoming harder with every second he spent in her company. He could be in real trouble.

CHAPTER EIGHT

SHE WAS REALLY in India. Her mother's homeland. She was finally here. She experienced a whole gamut of emotions in a matter of seconds. It still felt surreal, unbelievable. She pressed her hand against her chest, trying to ease the choked sensation, as if she wanted to cry and to laugh and to twirl all at the same time.

From Connor's warm expression, she could tell he could empathise with what she was experiencing, but she was grateful he knew to leave her the space to give in to her feelings.

The heat as they left the airport was the first sign she was in a completely different country. Ayun, the man who'd been sent by Connor's friend to meet them at Arrivals, ushered them towards a waiting car and they were soon on their way to their hotel. It was before sunrise, so the roads were clear.

Rina leaned forward to look out of the window, hoping for her first glimpse of India, but it was too dark to see anything beyond flickering lights.

'Try to stay awake until we get to the hotel,' Connor said. 'Then sleep as soon as you can. It will help you get adjusted to the time difference. Set your alarm for around nine-thirty a.m. You don't want to oversleep. It'll make the jetlag worse.'

Rina nodded. It all sounded like sensible advice. Apart from staying awake until they got to the hotel, she wasn't sure she would be able to follow any of it.

Part of her was desperate to wait and watch the sun rise over her first day in India. It was a romantic notion, but now that she'd got it into her head she couldn't let the idea go. She glanced over at Connor. After what he'd just suggested, it was unlikely he would agree to stay up with her.

For a moment she wished Aunt Maria was with her. She tried to work out what time it would be in Switzerland but, regardless of the hour, her aunt probably wouldn't answer her call anyway.

Rina sat down by the window in her hotel room. She hadn't spoken to her aunt since she left Switzerland. It was the longest they'd ever gone without speaking to each other. Surely Aunt Maria couldn't still be angry with her?

Usually any disagreements between them were resolved within a couple of days. Rina could understand if her aunt was disappointed in her, but all her life she'd done as her aunt wanted—stayed out of harm's way, stuck in her fairy tale tower.

Rina even understood why her aunt was so overprotective—she was all Aunt Maria had left in the world. But Rina didn't need or want to be sheltered all her life. Even at university her aunt had been there, and now, at the age of twenty-six, Rina needed this tiny taste of freedom. She craved the chance to do something for herself. Did that make her selfish? If so she would be selfish for a few more days. Then, afterwards, Rina would return to the tower and accept her daily life.

Her phone beeped. She hurried over, hoping it was her aunt, but was surprised and delighted to see the message was from Connor.

I know you're not sleeping. Why don't you come to my room? You'll be able to watch the sunrise much better from up here.

She laughed as she typed a reply, telling him she was on her way. It certainly didn't seem to her like an invitation from someone who only thought of her as a business colleague—

he knew her well enough to work out exactly what she'd planned.

Connor didn't speak as he opened the door to his room. The silence was almost reverential as they walked over to the large window. It was five a.m. and the sun was slowly beginning to rise.

She watched, breathless, as the golden rays slowly brought the awe and beauty of the Indian city of Bengaluru to light. She gave a quick glance to Connor. Seconds later he stood closer to her, placing a comforting arm around her, allowing her to lean back and rest her head against his shoulder as they both concentrated on the dawn.

She didn't know how long they stood there, silently seeing the city wake up, but the long journey was finally beginning to take its toll on her and she yawned. She felt the ghost of Connor's lips against her forehead.

'Come on,' he said. 'There's still time for you to get some rest before we start the day. I'll see you at breakfast.'

He went to hold the door open for her—an effective way to break whatever spell she'd been under, watching India come to life.

Back in her own room, as she braided her hair, she grimaced. It had been hot even when they'd arrived. If it was that hot now, before the day began, it was only going to get hotter as the day went on.

She didn't love the idea of the heavy weight of her hair plastered to her head in the heat. If only she didn't have to deal with it. She'd kept it long out of an unspoken love for her aunt. After her accident Rina had had to have her head shaved for surgeries. It had taken a while for her hair to grow back, and one of her earliest post-accident memories was of Aunt Maria gently brushing it and tying it into different styles. As she'd grown up, it had become a daily ritual for her aunt to brush her hair, and her aunt often used the time to tell Rina stories about her father and Lachance. Her aunt had told her often how much she loved the length and thickness of Rina's hair, and had always sounded upset if Rina even hinted at getting it cut.

But it had been a long time since her aunt had brushed her hair for her.

At breakfast, Connor outlined what he had planned for her for the day. They were staying two nights in Bengaluru before driving to Mysuru, where they would spend another three days before returning to Bengaluru for the first leg of their journey back to Switzerland.

Rina's mouth turned down. He was making it sound as if their time in India was almost over rather than just beginning. It was such a contrast to the warm man who'd stood with her as she'd watched the sun rise. Now he was all about work, emphasising how business travel was a whirlwind trip without much free time. Although that wasn't going to be the case for her.

'I've been doing some more research on the area,' she began, 'and I have a list of restaurants to visit and food I want to try. Ma used to make idli and dosas when I was younger, but I haven't had a good one in years so that's on my must-do list.'

Connor frowned. 'I'm not sure I'll have much time to take you.'

'That's okay. You don't have to take me.'

He closed his eyes. 'Are we going to have this argument again?'

Rina rolled her eyes. 'No argument. These places are for breakfast. I won't be going out at night.'

'You shouldn't go out alone in a place you don't know.'

She didn't know whether his concern was heart-warming or whether he was irritating in his over-protectiveness. She smiled, deciding to interpret it as a sign that he cared for her a little.

'I spoke to Ayun before I came down for breakfast. He called to check everything was okay with the room and said he's been told to make himself available for my convenience by your colleague. That's kind of them, isn't it? Anyway, he said he can take me to a restaurant tomorrow morning.'

Connor pressed his lips together.

'Oh, come on, Connor. You can't still be worried.'

'I don't know Ayun.'

'But your colleague does. He wouldn't arrange for someone untrustworthy to be responsible for me.'

Why was he being so difficult? If he hadn't drummed it into her that there could only be a business relationship between them she might almost believe he cared about her on a personal level.

She narrowed her eyes. 'Or is it me you don't trust?'

His lips quirked. 'You can be quite the handful.'

Rina huffed in mock offence. 'Nobody has ever said that about me before. I guess you bring out the worst in me. The question is, what do I bring out in you?' she asked, batting her eyelashes.

Connor splashed coffee on his hand. He blinked a couple of times. 'My sense of self-preservation,' he muttered under his breath.

She gave him a cheeky grin, then got up to return to her room and get ready to go into the office with him.

As she was twisting her hair up into a bun she thought again about how much it was getting in her way, with the humidity making it harder to deal with. Luckily, she had some Essence with her, but she still wanted to do something about the sheer weight of her hair. There was no reason for her to keep it that length any more. She loved her aunt, but she wasn't a young girl who needed to be controlled by her any more. Coming to India despite Aunt Maria's objections proved she was independent, and she could make her own decisions—particularly about her hair.

Before she met Connor she wandered along the hotel concourse to see what shops and services they had available, smiling when she saw a small hair salon. She walked in to see if there were any appointments available later that day.

The drive to the office was much slower than that from the airport. The sounds of horns and bicycle bells competed with loud voices.

Rina sat back in her seat with a huge smile.

'Has it sunk in yet?' Connor asked her with an indulgent grin.

How could he tell exactly what she was thinking?

'It's beginning to feel real. The sounds and smells are so unique.' She had the windows open and sniffed at the air. As she pulled her head back inside she plucked at her top. 'I may need to add buying some cotton clothes to my list, because otherwise I'm going melt into a puddle of sweat by mid-afternoon. Please tell me the office is air conditioned.'

'You'll be relieved to hear it is.'

'You know, my mum went to university in Switzerland, but she worked in IT. I think if she hadn't met my father she might have come back to India and settled in Bengaluru. It's strange to think she could have driven down these roads as a child.' Almost to herself, she added, 'I'm already starting to feel closer to her, just being in the same country.'

Connor covered her hand. He looked over at the driver and at Ayun before giving her hand a quick squeeze and letting go.

Before coming to India, Rina had wondered whether some of her old grief would return. She'd never got the chance to visit these places with her parents. Rina was sure her mother had planned to take her often, since she'd organised her entry card. But instead of grief, Rina felt a quiet sense of connection and belonging.

In some ways it was similar to the connection she'd felt with Connor the first time she'd met him. There'd been a sense of familiarity and recognition with him. It was completely separate to the physical attraction she'd also experienced, although that had been startling in its intensity.

She took a quick glance at Connor. Apart from brief moments when his natural empathy came through, he was trying hard to keep things between them businesslike. She didn't fully understand why. They had been developing a friendship—more than a friendship if she thought about their kiss, which she did far too often. But that was before he'd found out she was Maria Lachance's niece and before he found out the company he wanted to do business with was partly hers.

She had to find a way to bring them back to that easy-going relationship. That was all that was possible. At one point she had hoped there could be something more between them, but she wasn't being realistic. Not only did they live in different countries, but they also wanted different things from life. She wanted to explore the world, while Connor made it clear he viewed travel as a necessary evil.

A few hours later, Rina was beginning to feel that familiar sense of frustration. Connor seemed to be following her around as she toured the facilities and met the staff. Was he worried about what she would ask them or what they might tell her about working for Newmans? Or was he being protective? She didn't need someone looking out for her when she was inside the company buildings. He wasn't quite as bad as her aunt, but he was becoming close.

'Connor,' she said finally, after he'd moved her away from a large group of people who had surrounded her, interested to meet the lady from Lachance. 'Don't you have meetings to go to?'

He shook his head.

'Isn't Nihal waiting for you?' she asked.

'Not at the moment,' he replied.

'Well, don't you have some work waiting for you? Don't let me keep you from it.'

'You're not.'

She expelled an exasperated breath. 'If you want me to get a real view of Newmans, so I can use my influence on my aunt, then you need to let me go around on my own.'

He pressed his lips together. Then briefly inclined his head. 'Fine. Why don't you message me when you've finished your tour?'

'Oh, that's not necessary. I'm going back to the hotel in half an hour. I'll see you there for dinner.'

'I can come back with you.'

She narrowed her eyes, tempted to tell him he was almost as stifling as her aunt when he was acting like her keeper rather than a business colleague.

'It's fine, Connor,' she said, tersely. 'I'll see you at dinner.'

She was nervous enough about what she had planned. She didn't need Connor questioning her further. If there was the remotest chance he would try to talk her out of it she wasn't going to risk him finding out beforehand. It would be too easy for him to make her second-guess her decision, and this was something she needed to do for herself—a small but obvious sign of her growing independence.

After she'd spoken to some more of the workers at Newmans she went back to the hotel, heading straight for the hair salon.

'Are you sure you want to cut so much off?'

the stylist asked, running the full length of
Rina's wet hair through her fingers. 'You
can do it in degrees. Perhaps just a couple
of inches now? Are you sure you want it to
the nape?'

Rina took a deep breath. 'Yes—cut it all
off and donate it, as we talked about earlier.'

'All right.'

Rina shut her eyes tight as she felt the scissors touch her hair and, hearing the sound
of the first snip, she felt a sense of loss. Her
hair wasn't her identity, but it had been like
a comfort blanket for so long. But she was
committed now. She had to see this through.

Slowly she opened her eyes and watched as
the stylist continued cutting, the long tresses
piling at her feet.

It was done.

After a quick shower, Rina rushed down
to the foyer, eager to meet Connor for dinner.

'Hello,' she greeted him, as she saw him
waiting by the reception desk.

'Your hair!'

She started at Connor's exclamation.

'Oh, yes.'

She ran her hand across her nape. It felt
bare, and slightly cold. She was used to it
being covered by her hair, but she didn't miss

the weight that had fallen with each snip of the hairdresser's scissors.

'I had it all cut off. Do you like it?' She performed a slow turn.

Her smile fell at Connor's frozen expression.

'What's wrong? Why are you looking like that? Does it look really bad. I've never had my hair this short before, but I thought it suited me. Doesn't it?'

'You look fine,' he answered curtly. 'Let's go. The car's waiting.'

Rina's eyes smarted. Why had his reaction hurt so much? His opinion of her hairstyle didn't matter as long as she liked it. And she did.

She ran her hand across the back of her neck again. The short length would take some getting used to, but taking such a simple and yet big step such as having her hair cut made her feel independent, empowered, invincible. Ready to take on the world.

But first she had to face a meal with Connor.

Connor knew he was staring, but he couldn't get over the way Rina looked. All that beautiful hair—gone. It would take some getting used to. Of course she was still Rina. Still beautiful. But now she looked more delicate.

During dinner he'd been staring, but that

was partly because they were sitting opposite each other and it would have been rude and awkward if he'd avoided looking at her. Now, after their meal, they'd decided to take a walk in the grounds of the hotel and, despite a Herculean effort on his part, he still wasn't able to keep his eyes off her.

'I'm still me, Connor,' she said, unconsciously echoing his thoughts.

'You, but different.'

'A new me, then.'

'What made you decide to have it cut? I know you're impulsive, but I have to admit I am a little shocked.'

'It wasn't really impulsive. My hair has been weighing me down for a while.' She paused, and with a giggle added, 'Physically and metaphorically. It was time to do something about it.'

'When was the last time you cut your hair?'

'I've never really had it cut before, just trimmed the ends to keep them tidy.'

'That's a drastic change, then.'

'Hmm, I'm not sure about *drastic*. I think the correct word is necessary.'

She sounded happy, and free, as if the loss of her hair really had lightened her. He hoped she wouldn't regret it and become upset later.

'Don't worry, I'm not going to lie awake crying about how I've lost my beautiful hair.'

How was she reading his mind?

'Was it really that much of a nuisance?' he asked.

'When you're trying to stand but your head gets wrenched back because you've accidentally sat on your own hair, even once, is one time too many.'

He couldn't help laughing at the image her rueful confession conjured.

'How do you think your aunt's going to react?' he asked.

'Surprised, I guess.'

She sounded blasé, but he already knew how much she loved her aunt and cared about her opinion.

'It's going to be strange for you now, working on hair products. You were a walking advert for Essence before.'

Rina gave him a cheeky smirk. 'Everybody who uses Essence is a walking advert for it.'

He inclined his head, captivated by her easy wit.

'Anyway,' she continued, 'Essence works on short hair just as well as long—as you should know.'

He inhaled sharply when she touched his own wavy strands.

'How did you know I use Essence?' he asked.

'I can always tell. Like I said, it shows.'

'Ah, so you judge people on their hair?'

Her laughter trilled out. 'No, only people from companies that want to buy Essence. It's an easy way to weed only those who are only interested in the money they can make from the product but don't care about Essence itself, or the ethos of Lachance.'

It was the perfect segue into a conversation about business, but Connor was reluctant to follow that path. In fact, he was finding that Rina was distracting him from business. He had spent most of the day accompanying her while she toured the company's facilities, which had been completely unnecessary. He could have come up with a million reasons for his actions, but the simple truth was that he had wanted to see the company through her eyes—see her face light up when she met people or learned something new, listen to her perceptive observations, hear her tinkling laugh and feel it cheering his soul.

He stiffened. They were business colleagues. Regardless of how enticing she was, he had to forget the first couple of days they had spent together and flirtatiously got to know each other and maintain a professional distance.

'Time to head inside,' he said abruptly, and slightly more harshly than he'd intended, judging from her expression. 'There's lots to do tomorrow.'

He walked her to the lifts in the foyer, but couldn't risk being in a small, enclosed space with her so told he needed to speak to someone at Reception and walked away, knowing she was looking after him until the lift doors closed.

He knew he was sending mixed messages, but despite his best efforts he couldn't maintain the necessary distance between them.

The next morning, Connor positioned himself near the reception desk in the hotel foyer. From his vantage point he could see the lifts and the stairs, so there was no possibility he would miss Rina when she came down.

He glanced at his watch. She was ten minutes late. She couldn't have already left, could she? She'd promised she wouldn't go out on her own. She was impulsive, but not reckless. He looked at the door. Should he call Ayun to make sure he hadn't met Rina?

'Connor! Morning. I didn't expect to see you down here. Is your driver late?'

As he turned towards Rina's voice he was again taken aback by her changed appearance— and by the realisation the urge to run his fingers through her hair hadn't gone away.

'Connor, are you okay?' Rina asked, with a look of concern.

'I'm fine.'

She gave him a relieved smile. 'That's good.' She looked towards the door. 'Have you seen Ayun? I'm running a little late, so I thought he'd be here by now.'

'I asked him not to come.'

'Why would you do that, Connor? Do you still think I'm being reckless?'

'No!' He hurried to reassure her. 'I mean *I'm* going to take you to breakfast.'

Her mouth dropped open. 'I thought you had back-to-back visits and meetings today.'

'And it's good to start a busy day with a big breakfast.'

Rina's grin was worth the adjustment to his schedule—although he still didn't fully understand his urge to change his plans. He'd felt guilty that he had spoilt their evening by being abrupt with her. Although there couldn't be a romantic relationship between them, there was no reason their business relationship couldn't be on cordially friendly terms.

He hadn't have to treat her as a stranger. He certainly didn't see her that way.

'Shall we go?' he asked, putting a gently guiding hand to the small of her back.

The breakfast café was busy, but the owner quickly cleared a table for them inside, under a ceiling fan.

Rina waved a hand in front of her face. 'Wow, I can't believe it's so hot so early. Thank goodness we've got the breeze.'

Connor nodded. 'Are you sure you want something hot to eat?' he asked.

'I definitely need to try the dosas, and I doubt it will be any cooler another day while we're in India, so now's as good a time as any.' She turned the menu over, looking through the options. 'Have you eaten here before?'

'Not at this restaurant. I eat idli and dosa fairly regularly, though. There's a really good takeaway restaurant near where I live in London.'

Rina raised her eyebrows. What had he said that surprised her?

In an effort to avoid getting caught up in her penetrating gaze, he stared at his menu.

'If you haven't tried dosa before I would recommend getting a plain one, or maybe a masala dosa,' he said. 'If you like cheese, then the cheese masala dosas are usually good.'

'What about idli? Do you have a recommendation?'

'I like sambar idli—but again, if you haven't tried them before, then perhaps plain idli would be the safest option.'

'I'm not sure I like taking the safest option...'

This time it was Connor who raised his eyebrows and released a sigh of resignation.

'I mean in my food choices,' Rina explained with a small laugh. 'I promise you I'm not going to take risks with my safety while I'm here.'

He wondered if she was beginning to regret coming with him on his business trip. She was seeing more of his offices than of the city.

A waiter came over to take their order, asking them about where they came from and what they were doing in the area. When he heard it was Rina's first time in Bengaluru, he offered suggestions for places she had to visit.

'Everyone is so friendly here,' Rina commented.

Connor looked at the other patrons. 'I would guess we're the only tourists they've had here for some time.'

Rina followed his gaze. 'Well, if they're

mostly locals here, that's a good sign the food is tasty.'

They didn't have long to wait for their food. This time it was the owner who stopped to chat with them.

Connor observed the interaction between him and Rina. She was probably completely unaware how much her bubbly and engaging personality contributed to the friendliness she received from the people around her.

Now Rina leaned over her plate and inhaled deeply. She gave a small moan which caused an immediate reaction in his body. Would she moan like that in bed with their bodies joined? Or would her moans be breathy, sultry or piercing?

He cleared his throat.

She looked up at him. 'Am I drooling?' she asked, wiping her hand across her mouth and picking up her first dosa.

'I can ask for cutlery if you prefer,' he offered.

Rina's mouth opened in mock horror. 'Not at all! I wouldn't think of using cutlery. Please tell me you're not the kind of person who uses a fork and knife to eat their pizza.'

He lifted his hand up. 'I wouldn't think of it.'

He felt as if he'd smiled more in the few

days he'd known Rina than he had in the rest of his life.

He picked up his dosa and then, apart from some appreciative noises from Rina as she dug into her food, they ate in relative silence.

'Oh, that was so good,' Rina said when they'd finished. She sat back in her chair and patted her stomach. 'I don't think I'll need to eat for the rest of the day.'

Her action brought his attention to her flat stomach and curvy hips. He turned to signal for the bill before his eyes were tempted to linger on her too long.

'Are you going to the office now?' she asked once they had left the café. 'I don't know what you arranged with Ayun. Is he meeting me back at the hotel or should I go with you?'

'Weren't you planning to come to the office today?'

'I thought I'd do a bit of sightseeing before our appointment at the distribution centre. Ayun was going to accompany me, but I don't know if he's returned to work. I don't want to disrupt him unnecessarily.'

Rina chewed on her bottom lip, a habit he'd noticed she had whenever she was weighing up her options, particularly those which might impose on other people. He could tell she really wanted to explore the city but, maybe partly because of his concerns, she didn't want to go on her own.

'Why don't we both go to the office now?' he said. 'I'll speak to Nihal about bringing the visit forward and then I can sort out a tour of Bengaluru for you.'

She bit her bottom lip again.

'Don't worry—it won't inconvenience anyone. The meeting I had with the London office immediately before our scheduled visit has been postponed, so I would be twiddling my thumbs during that time anyway.'

Rina smiled with relief. 'Oh, that's good. If you're sure?'

Connor gave a brisk nod. He *was* sure— at least he would be once he'd contacted the London office to excuse himself from that meeting. It was a regular weekly meeting with his core team and, since they were expecting him to be on leave this week anyway, they could hold it without him.

When they got to the office building, one of the people Rina had met the previous day came to greet her and lead her away. He called after her to remind her of the time they would have to meet to leave for the distribution centre visit, her thumbs up being all he got in acknowledgement.

* * *

Later that evening, Connor and Rina went to Nihal's home for dinner with him and his wife Mausami, but it was ridiculous how much Connor wanted to talk to Rina alone. He'd almost been tempted to get out of this dinner, so he could spend some time with her, but that would have been even more ridiculous.

'It's a shame you had to reschedule your holiday,' Nihal said. 'Rohan mentioned you were planning to visit him.'

'Yes, I thought I'd spend a few days with him before I came to see you, but plans changed.'

Connor gave a meaningful glance in Rina's direction. She had been chatting away to Mausami, but now she turned to him and gave him a quizzical look. He shrugged and shook his head briefly, and she turned back to her conversation. Had she sensed he was looking in her direction? Or had she been tuning into his conversation? He had to admit he'd kept one ear on what she was saying.

He noticed Nihal's small smile as he followed the direction of Connor's gaze. It wasn't the first time that evening his friend had caught him looking at Rina.

'I haven't seen Rohan since his wedding,' Connor continued.

'Really? So you didn't go to the—?'

'No, I was in Australia on business and couldn't get away.'

'Well, you missed an extravaganza.'

'Hey, guys,' Mausami said, coming to stand next to her husband. 'Do you want to play a board game. Rina said she hasn't played one since she was a child.'

Connor agreed immediately, although board games weren't usually his thing. If Rina hadn't played a board game for years it was probably because she didn't have any people her age to play with, stuck in Lachance tower with her aunt.

The four of them were soon laughing and bantering over the game until it was time to return to their hotel.

'I've had a lovely evening,' Rina said when she was in the car next to him. 'Your friends are wonderful. I like them so much. Thank you for inviting me along.'

'It's my pleasure. And they really liked you too.'

In fact he'd been shocked at how easily she'd got along with Nihal and Mausami. Although she had been friendly with the people she'd met at Newmans, she'd maintained a slight professional distance, maybe even some reserve, since she clearly wasn't used to meeting so many people. But with Mausami and Nihal she'd been engaging and witty and vivacious, and she'd won them over as quickly as she had him.

'You never mentioned you knew Nihal before. You made it sound like you met him through work.'

'Nihal is one of my closest friends. I've known him for years. We met at university.'

'Hmm…'

'What's that sound for?'

'I don't know. I guess for some reason I thought you didn't have any close relationships.'

Connor pressed his lips together. 'I have a few close friendships that I've had for years. But I don't have long-lasting relationships with women, if that's what you're referring to.'

'Why not?'

Connor was silent for a moment. The topic was completely unsuitable for people with a business relationship, but that evening the four of them had been a group of young people relaxing and having fun together, so perhaps it was natural for Rina to treat him accordingly. And perhaps it wasn't a bad thing to make it clear to Rina that any romantic relationship with him was impossible.

'I met Nihal through Rohan. Rohan was in my tutor group at uni. I was never close to anyone before then, apart from my brother and sister. We moved around too much when I was a child. It was better not to get close to anyone.'

Rina's forehead wrinkled. 'I don't understand. What do you mean, you moved around too much?'

Connor sighed. 'My dad found it difficult to hold a down a job, so we had to move around the country a lot to wherever he could find work. When I was a teenager there was one time I found myself getting close to a girl, and we tried to date. But then my family had to move suddenly. She wanted to stay in touch, but I couldn't see the point. We would be living miles away, I wouldn't have the money to go back to see her, and my family wouldn't have the space for her to visit me. So it ended. Since then I've kept any relationship very short term.'

'Because you travel for work a lot.'

Connor wasn't sure whether it was a question or a statement. 'Partly,' he said, although that wasn't the reason at all.

All the women he'd dated previously had been interested only in their career, and hadn't been looking for a long-term relationship, just occasional companionship—which was exactly what he wanted too. He'd never met anyone who'd made him believe commitment was something he could do.

'What about you?' he asked. 'Have you had any long-term relationships?'

Rena giggled. 'No. It's a bit tricky when you have an overprotective aunt. I've been on some dates, but nothing really developed. I've never met anyone I wanted to introduce to my aunt—it didn't seem fair to put anybody under such scrutiny. But I do hope to meet someone and get married someday, to somebody who understands that I need to stay with my aunt. Although that's probably unrealistic.'

Even in the darkness he could tell her face had fallen. He wished she would find a man who could make her dreams come true. But that man wasn't him.

CHAPTER NINE

RINA TRIED TO act nonchalant as the car approached Mysuru. With every mile they covered, they were a mile closer to the place her mother had lived for the first ten years of her life. Perhaps Rina would finally find the connection to her mother she had longed for.

She glanced over at Connor. As usual, he was scrolling through his tablet, writing notes. His face when he was concentrating was now so familiar and endearing to her. She wanted to reach out and run her finger along the furrows on his forehead.

If she was thinking about connections, she'd also like to rediscover the connection she'd felt with Connor when they first met. She still loved spending time with him, sharing her thoughts, hearing his opinions. But there was a distance between them now. He was sticking to his plan to maintain a business relationship—for the most part.

Occasionally the Connor from the rampion field reappeared. And she adored it. Because she knew without any shred of doubt *that* was the natural Connor. He was forcing himself to be aloof and maintain a professional distance. If only she could convince him it wasn't necessary.

'Are you sure you don't want to come to the office with me?' Connor asked.

'I'm sure, thanks. Unless you think I need to go?'

He pressed his lips together. 'It was your suggestion to see Newmans' facilities, not mine.'

Rina bit the inside of her cheek. She supposed she shouldn't be surprised he was still irritated that she'd forced him to accompany her to India.

She beamed at him, as if she hadn't noticed his grumpy attitude. 'I think I've got a good idea of how your company functions by now. Thanks. I'm very impressed.'

Even if she hadn't already promised him, she would have definitely tried to convince her aunt they should accept his company's proposal based on what she'd seen. Regardless of how much she liked Connor on a personal level, she would encourage her aunt because she was convinced, with everything she'd seen so far, that it would be the best business decision for Essence.

That was if Aunt Maria ever spoke to her again. She hadn't returned any of her messages. It was the only low point of the entire trip, but Rina still couldn't regret her decision to seize what might be her only opportunity to visit Mysuru.

'I'll be fine with Ayun. If you're sure you won't need him?'

Newmans had assigned Ayun to stay with them until they left Karnataka. Although technically he was supposed to be available for Connor's needs, they all knew Newmans would agree to anything Rina requested, so Ayun had said he would accompany her while she explored Mysuru.

Rina did feel a slight twinge of guilt that the company was going out of its way to make sure she was happy.

It had come as a surprise when Connor hadn't protested at her plans to go around without him. Perhaps she had misjudged him as being overprotective when he really wasn't.

Besides, Ayun was only going to be with her for the day. The following day she was hoping that Mausami would be able to come up to spend some time with her. They'd got on like a house on fire during dinner the previous evening, and had made plans to see each other again. Mausami worked for an IT company and was able to set her own hours, so she'd told Rina she was going to take the day off.

After having so few friendships while she was growing up, it was a blessing for Rina to find someone she got on so well with. But it made Rina realise how different her instantaneous connection with Connor had been. She couldn't pretend that she hadn't found him incredibly attractive from the moment he'd turned round in the rampion field. And while their friendship developed, her attraction to him kept on growing.

She hadn't wanted to say goodbye to him after showing him around Lake Thun. It had seemed as if all the pieces were falling into place when he'd told he was travelling to India.

But since then she'd felt like a yo-yo—bouncing back and forth between wanting to explore having something more with Connor or maintaining a friendship.

In a way, Connor had taken some of the decision away from her, by trying to adopt a business-only attitude. It was almost as though he'd drawn an indelible line between the couple who'd shared a passionate goodbye kiss and the couple they were now. But there were times when he looked at her with such intensity, he still had to feel something more than business.

She liked him. A lot. But she knew as well as Connor did that there was no future for them. She could never leave her aunt for good and she doubted Connor would leave England for Switzerland. It was clear to her they wanted different things out of life; their dreams were not the same. She wasn't so naive as not to realise that.

Calls and car horns broke her out of her introspection and she realised they were already in Mysuru. She laughed to herself. She had almost expected a huge sign welcoming her—some kind of fanfare heralding this actualisation of a dream. But visiting the place where her mum had been born and raised wasn't a big deal to anyone but her. No need for fanfares.

After dropping Connor off at the Newmans office, Rina went with Ayun to look at some temples. But although on any other day the unique structures stretching to the sky would have had her brimming full of ideas, it didn't take her long to realise it wasn't what she really wanted to do. She was desperate to see the house her mother had grown up in. Perhaps even go to the park where her grandfather had pushed her mother on the swings.

Sometimes the stories her mother had told her—as few as they'd been—seemed like something from a dream. Rina wasn't sure how much she could rely on her memories from sixteen years ago.

Rina's mood deflated further when Mausami called to let her know she hadn't been able to get time off work because an emergency had cropped up, but she tried to keep the disappointment out of her voice as they made arrangements to meet up when Rina returned to Bengaluru before she took her flight back home.

After she left the temple Ayun recommended a nearby public garden which had beautiful flower beds and said there would be benches. She wasn't sure whether or not that was his subtle way of indicating he needed a rest, but she agreed.

Once she found a free bench, Ayun handed her a drink and then moved away to speak on his phone.

She tried to concentrate on the beauty of her surroundings, but she was thinking about how her plans for the following day would need to change now Mausami wouldn't be there. Although she was sure Nihal would agree to Ayun accompanying her again, she was also sure he wasn't excited about playing chaperone to a tourist. But from what she now knew she doubted Connor would be happy with her going out alone.

She had wanted someone with her for moral support when she visited her mum's childhood places. She didn't want to put Ayun, lovely as he was, in an awkward position if she happened to get emotional.

'What's wrong?' a familiar voice called out.

She looked up in shock as Connor walked towards her with a concerned expression. He was so perceptive…always surprisingly attuned to her feelings. There was no point pretending everything was okay.

'Mausami can't come up. Didn't Nihal tell you?'

'Yes, that's why I came. I wanted to see how you were, since I knew you'd be upset once you heard the news.'

Rina pouted. Why did he have to be so kind? Every time she'd convinced herself there was no future for her and Connor, he did something to show he must care about her and started her hoping all over again.

She reminded herself of all the reasons they couldn't be together. They were on different paths in life. He lived in England. She couldn't move away from her aunt. He wanted to stay grounded and she wanted to explore the world. He couldn't make a commitment. At least, he'd convinced himself he couldn't—and who was she to say he was wrong?

Although in so many ways she felt as though Connor knew her better than almost anyone else, and she wanted to believe he'd let her get to know him on a profound level, the reality was they'd only known each other a week. And she wasn't ready to move her world to his—not that he'd ever indicated he wanted her to.

Connor couldn't quite interpret Rina's expression. Surprise, naturally. Pleasure? He hoped so. But there was something else too.

'You came here because you thought I'd be upset? What about your meeting?' she asked.

'It finished quicker than I expected, so I decided to leave work early and join you on your tour. I've managed to get everything I needed done today, so now I'm at your disposal.'

She didn't know he'd condensed everything into one meeting as soon as he'd found out Mausami wasn't able to come and spend time with Rina.

'What?'

This time her expression made him laugh. 'I'm going to be your guide. I took the rest of today and tomorrow off. I was supposed to be on holiday this week, so it wasn't a problem.'

'Didn't you have plans to go somewhere? I thought I heard you were hoping to meet your friend? Rohan I think you called him.'

Connor realised that although she'd been chatting with Mausami, Rina had clearly had one ear on Connor's conversation with Nihal.

'There isn't enough time for me to fly to Rohan's island. I can visit him another time.'

'Rohan's island? Your friend has his own *island*?' Rina asked with a laugh.

'Not technically. But he is the King.'

Rina blinked. She stared at him, furrowing her brow, as if she was trying to work out if he was serious.

'Your friend Rohan, the man you were swapping stories with Nihal about, is a king?'

'That's right. I was invited to his coronation, but I couldn't make it.' His lips quirked. 'What's was on your list of places to visit?'

'The palace, of course—I still haven't done that. And tomorrow I planned to see the sculpture museum. Mausami also suggested I go to one of the silk markets.'

'Are you ready to leave? The car's waiting.'

She grabbed her handbag and cotton covering, but didn't say anything else until they were in the car.

'I'm not sure which is harder to believe, that your friend is a king or that you've taken time off.'

He rolled his eyes. 'I do have a life outside work.'

She quirked an eyebrow. 'Really? Do you? Not from what you've told me. It's movies, books and cooking—no socialising.'

'Perhaps I haven't told you everything I do in my spare time.' He waggled his eyebrows suggestively.

She made a spluttering sound. 'But would you be doing this if not for me?'

He grimaced. If Mausami had been able to come he probably wouldn't have taken the time off. But Rina would feel guilty if he admitted that. And, if he was being strictly truthful with himself, a part of him had been pleased when he heard Mausami couldn't make it. He enjoyed spending time with Rina and there wouldn't be many opportunities to do so going forward.

He'd already decided it would be a bad idea to keep in touch with Rina after she'd returned to Switzerland. If she kept her promise and managed to persuade her aunt to go into business with Newmans he would still be involved with Lachance Boutique in obtaining the licence for Essence. But Rina was the product developer—there would be no reason for her to be involved with those details.

But that would be after they'd returned to Switzerland. They still had a few days in India and then the long journey back. After that they wouldn't be in each other's futures—it wouldn't be fair of him to keep in contact with her when he couldn't offer her any kind of permanence. But as long as he was honest with her why shouldn't he enjoy the time he had with her in the present?

Connor was content to follow Rina round as she toured Mysuru Palace. She barely spent seconds viewing some of the architecture, but then spent long minutes with her notebook out, looking at pieces that seemed to him exactly the same as the ones that hadn't held her interest.

Looking inside her notebook would be a fascinating insight into Rina's mind, Connor felt a strange pang in his chest—a pervading sense of loss that he would never be the one she shared her notebook with.

The next day they went to Brindavan Garden, followed by the Mysuru Sand Sculpture Museum, before driving to a street bazaar.

Rina rushed from stall to stall, reaching out to run an admiring hand along the bales of silk, lifting some towards the sun, laughing as she chatted to the stallholders.

He walked over to her. 'Please, let me try bargaining for anything you want to buy.'

She shook her head. 'It seems wrong. Putting it in perspective, it's not as if they're charging outrageous starting prices. I know they expect bargaining when they name their price, but it seems unnecessary to me.'

He laughed ruefully. Why had he expected anything different?

'Oh, that's the place Mausami mentioned. Let's go,' she said, grabbing his forearm.

Inside the stall Rina looked over the ready-made salwar and kurtas. She reached up to touch the occasional sleeve or hem of an outfit worn by the mannequins, then looked at the clothes on the shelves to see if she could find the same garment.

It wasn't like a department store, where you could find the same outfit in different sizes. It was rare that the same material would have been used more than once, let alone in a variety of sizes.

She made a beeline for the sarees. 'How gorgeous is this colour?' she asked him.

She held it against her arm, where the pink

hues of the material brought out the peach tones of her skin. She would look absolutely stunning in any outfit in that colour. He wanted to rush over and buy huge quantities.

'And it feels so wonderful,' she said, as she ran her fingers over the material. 'I would love to somehow recreate this sensation in a Lachance product.'

Connor gave her a confused look. 'How would you do that?'

'Here—feel this.' She grabbed his hand and ran it with hers over the silk. 'This is how your hair should feel after washing and using a treatment,' she continued. 'I want to capture the same rich, luxurious experience when people use a product.'

He became conscious they were still holding hands and released her reluctantly. 'It sounds like India is inspiring you—as you hoped.'

She nodded, her eyes bright. 'It's amazing. I've been under such a dry spell recently, but now I feel like I'm in a monsoon of ideas. I've made so many notes! Not only ideas for products but for new containers, and there's even a new method I want to experiment with.'

'A new method?'

She pressed her lips together. 'Lots of ideas.' Then, clearly changing the subject, she said,

'There are so many beautiful sarees. I wish I had the chance to wear them. But maybe more opportunities will come if I buy the sarees first.'

'I don't think that's how it works,' he said, with a dry tone.

'Yes, I know… I know. You don't believe in fate or destiny—you think it's coincidence. And I'm sure you don't believe in manifesting. But "there are more things in Heaven and Earth, Connor, than are dreamt of in your philosophy."'

'Pardon?'

'Hamlet.'

'Okay…'

Her mind was an enigma—one he wanted to unravel almost as much as he would love to unravel Rina wearing a saree…

He blinked at the direction of his thoughts. He might have decided to enjoy his time in her company but he still needed to maintain a distance. 'Perhaps you can buy a few sarees for inspiration at Lachance.'

'That's a brilliant idea!'

The smile she gave him took his breath away.

'Perhaps we should carry on looking at the other stalls?' he suggested, deliberately walking away from her.

She was far too fetching, and if he didn't move he would give in to the temptation to gather her to him and press his lips to hers, regardless of how public the setting was. But he wouldn't move too fast—he didn't want to lose track of her in the crowd.

After they'd finished at the bazaar they stopped at a café for a cold drink and some snacks.

'Where's next on your list?' Connor asked.

Rina bit her lip. Why was she looking nervous?

'What's up?' he asked.

'I told you my mum lived in Mysuru until she was ten, didn't I?' she asked. When he nodded, she continued, 'I'd like to go to the area she lived in. Perhaps even find the house. But it won't be interesting for you.'

'I would enjoy going with you, if you don't mind,' he replied softly. Although she hadn't mentioned it yesterday, he knew she wanted to visit her mother's former home.

'Are you sure?' she asked, her relief visible. 'Yes.'

She smiled, but there was a small, almost imperceptible tension in her mouth. She was worried about the visit. He imagined it would be overwhelming to finally have the chance to go somewhere your heart had longed to see. A place that had great significance for her mother—a chance for a connection with the person Rina had missed since she was young girl.

He probably would have gone with her for support even if Mausami had come up. He wanted to be there for her, even though he would never tell her his reasoning—she might be able to work out that he cared about her if he told her.

'Let's go back to the car and we can head there now,' he said, instinctively holding out his hand.

She grabbed it with a grateful smile, then she took a deep breath and they walked to the car.

'Can I help you?'

Rina turned from the gate enclosing what had once been her mother's home to see a woman, perhaps the age her parents would have been, speaking to her.

Since she'd asked in English, Rina replied in the same language, rather than attempting to speak in Kannada.

'Oh, I'm just looking at the house here. My mother grew up on this road, but I don't know if the houses have been rebuilt since she was here.'

'No, I grew up here too, and my mother still lives next door. The houses are exactly the same.'

Rina turned to Connor with a huge smile. 'So my mother did live in that exact house. She went through that door and looked out of those windows.'

'What was your mother's name? Maybe I remember her,' the woman said.

When Rina told her, the woman smiled warmly. 'I *do* remember her. Your mother was the same age as me. We played together all the time and walked to school together. I was sad when she left. I think when we were nine or ten?'

Rina nodded. Meeting someone who'd spent time with her mother, perhaps shared stories and secrets and wishes for the future, was surreal. She wanted to ask the woman to tell her everything.

'I can't believe I'm seeing her daughter,' the woman continued. 'How is she?'

Rina's sorrow was echoed in the woman's face when she heard about Rina's mother's passing.

'My name is Urmi. If you have time, why don't you come inside? I know there will be some photos of me playing with Riya. And my mother is always telling me about what the two of us used to get up to, if you want to hear her stories.'

Rina blinked back the sudden rush of moisture in her eyes as she tried to absorb this offer to see childhood photos of her mum and hear what she'd been like when she was younger. Even hearing her mother's name, Riya, spoken so easily.

She sensed Connor coming to stand next to her, offering silent comfort and support. She swallowed. 'I would love to do that, if you're sure we won't be disturbing you.'

'Not at all. Unfortunately, the people who live in Riya's old house aren't here for a few days, otherwise I'm sure they would have showed you around. You don't live in India do you?'

'No, I live in Switzerland.'

Urmi's eyebrows rose. 'I see. And is this your husband?' she asked, looking at Connor.

'No, Connor's a work colleague. We actually came to Mysuru on business.'

'Well, please, both of you, come inside.'

Rina took a step forward, then halted. She looked through the bags Connor was carrying for her and pulled out a box of mithai. She couldn't go into the lady's house empty-handed.

Before long they were sitting with Urmi

and her mother, enjoying tea and snacks. And hours later Rina walked back out onto her mother's childhood street in a daze, still trying to process everything she'd been told and store it in her memory for ever.

'Are you okay?' Connor asked, resting his hand on her arm.

She nodded, unable to speak.

He gathered her into his arms, holding her tight. She leaned into him, soaking up his wordless support. He made her feel safe and protected, secure and brave enough to process how she was feeling. She only wished he could always be there for her in situations like this, and she also wished she could be the one to offer *him* strength and support whenever he needed it.

She'd been without her parents for sixteen years. She'd had to get used to a new normal at an early age, leaving the home she'd grown up in and moving to a different country. Just as her mother had left India, at a similar age, to move to England.

She slowly became aware of looks from passers-by.

'I'm okay. Thank you. Thanks for coming with me,' she said.

'Of course.'

He reached out to hold her hand as they

walked back to the car, where Connor gave the instruction to head back to the hotel.

Part of her felt bad that she was cutting the day short, but she knew Connor wouldn't mind, because he was accompanying her rather than visiting somewhere on his own accord. She needed to take some time to re-calibrate. She had never expected to meet anyone who had actually known her mother. When it came to her father, Aunt Maria was able to share many stories of him growing up, but there had been nobody to tell her stories about her mum until today.

When they reached the hotel, Connor turned to her. 'Do you want to have a cup of tea or something to eat?' he asked.

She shook her head. 'I think I want to take a rest.'

They walked to the lifts. To her surprise, Connor got out on her floor and walked with her to her room.

He didn't follow her inside, but remained in the doorway.

She tried to smile, but knew her effort was weak from the concern in his eyes.

'I'm okay, Connor. You don't have to worry about me. I'm actually really happy.' She reached out to squeeze his hand and reas-sure him.

He leant forward to press a kiss against her forehead. 'Do you want to be alone, or can I stay here with you?'

Suddenly being alone was the last thing she wanted. She knew Connor wouldn't pester her with questions or even force a conversation. He was exactly who she needed to be with at that moment.

She nodded for him to come in. 'Why don't I order some tea and food to my room?'

At his nod, she went to the phone to place her order, then went to stand in front of the window while they waited for their food to arrive. As she'd expected, Connor came over to stand next to her. She put her hand in his. Then she made some small talk about the view until there was the knock at the door.

'Do your parents live near you, Connor?' she asked once they'd started eating.

She noticed his grip tighten on the cup handle and wondered whether she'd upset him with her question. He'd mentioned his brother and sister, and how his father hadn't kept a job for long so they'd always moved around, but she couldn't recall him saying much else about his parents. Were they still around?

'I keep a home for my parents in England. Norfolk. Do you know it?'

'The bump on the east coast?'

He smiled. 'That's right. It's in a place called Cromer, near the beach.'

'Is that where you grew up?'

His mouth tightened. 'As I told you, I grew up all over the place. We rarely stayed anywhere for long. Even now, my parents are travelling round the world. They don't even tell us where they are. But I bought them a base where they can stay if they are ever in the country.'

'And where do your brother and sister live?'

'Both of them live in London. North of the river.'

'The River Thames?'

He smiled again. 'That's right. Sometimes I forget you don't live in England.'

'Well, I did live there until I was ten.'

The stories she'd heard of her mother came rushing back to her mind. Rina had grown up with a loving aunt, and would describe her youth as happy. But she had never admitted how much she missed her parents…missed her mother. More now than ever.

She shut her eyes tight, overwhelmed and exhausted by the intensity of her emotions.

'I think I'm going to lie down for a bit,' she said, standing up and heading to the bed.

'Good idea,' Connor replied, standing up too.

'Would you...?' Rina began, before tailing off.

'Would I what?' Connor asked in a gentle tone.

'Would you stay and lie next to me for a little bit?'

She needed the comfort of Connor's presence. Wanted the strength of his arms.

He paused for a moment, then with a slight inclination of his head, he walked to the side of the bed and took off his shoes.

They both lay on the bed, facing each other. Connor traced the contours of her face with his fingertip. He leaned over to gently press his lips against hers, then turned onto his back and held out his arms. Rina lay against him and closed her eyes.

He heard her breathing change and saw the gentle rise and fall of her chest, relieved that she'd finally fallen asleep in his arms. He fought the temptation to stay next to her, perhaps even join her for a short nap. Carefully, he drew his arms away, anxious not to wake her. He looked down at her, desperate to press his lips against hers but knowing it was a bad idea. Instead, he rose off the bed.

He'd never felt this way before. Their closeness went beyond a physical attraction. It made him wary, made him want to put up his defence shield.

Should he return to his own room? He looked over at her sleeping figure. After the day she'd had he didn't want her to be alone when she woke up. He briefly went to his room to fetch his laptop and then returned to hers. He wanted to be there in case she needed him—for anything.

When Rina finally woke up it was already dark outside. She looked peaceful, but drained. He suggested they order a meal from Room Service. While they ate he kept the conversation neutral, not wanting to talk about Lachance Boutique or Newmans but letting her know she could talk to him about her mother, her family, if she wanted.

CHAPTER TEN

RINA WAS SILENT on the car ride back to Bengaluru. She had chatted with Connor over breakfast that morning, but there was something forced in her smile. Was she as confused as he was about their closeness the previous evening? Or was she thinking about her mum?

The previous day had clearly taken an emotional toll on Rina. He tried to empathise with what she must be going through. Rina's mother sounded so much like her. He might not have the best or even a good relationship with his parents, especially with his father, but he couldn't imagine growing up without them.

The original plan had been to spend a few days in Mysuru and then a few more in Bengaluru before flying home to Europe. But he'd decided to take some more leave for the rest of his time in India, rearranged some things, and added a stop in Mumbai to their plans.

Rina's face when he'd told her had held the first genuine smile he'd seen.

They'd decided to head back to Bengaluru after breakfast, since Rina hadn't done much sightseeing on their previous visit.

When they got there their first stop was Tipu Sultan's Summer Palace. At first he wasn't sure whether that was a wise decision. Would it bring back memories of Tipu Sultan's Mysuru Palace, which they'd visited just before going to her mother's place the previous day? But the building seemed to help Rina's high spirits return. She was back to being curious about everything, with endless questions and insightful observations.

As they wandered around Rina would occasionally stop and take out her notebook, making a quick note or sketching some of the shapes she was looking at. He couldn't imagine how she found new things to add to her notebook after they'd already visited the other palace. But then, he didn't have the same kind of creative mind as Rina.

In some ways they had their devotion to work in common. Rina was always thinking about Lachance Boutique—the products she could develop and the improvements she could make. Perhaps it was because it was her family's company. Connor hoped her aunt would come to understand Rina's need to leave her everyday surroundings once in a while. He was sure she would—this inspired Rina was something to behold.

Passion for work. Passion for life. He couldn't stop his mind from wondering what her passion in bed would be like. Based on their kisses, she would be dynamite. He wished he could blame the sultry heat for the nature of his thoughts. But it wasn't to blame.

Rina was superlative—that was the only way he could think to describe her. And he wanted her. Wanted her in his arms, in his bed, underneath him.

But that was impossible. Apart from the fact she wanted to experience more than her hometown, and he wanted to travel as little as possible, his experience showed him he wasn't good at making commitments. The nomadic nature of his upbringing made him incapable of forming long-term attachments. Or perhaps he wouldn't have been a relationship kind of person regardless of his childhood. No one he'd previously dated had managed to keep his attention, and he always began to get bored quickly and want to move on—possibly the way his parents did. Only for him it was women rather than places.

He couldn't imagine getting bored with

Rina—she was too engaging, too interesting. But that didn't change his intrinsic nature. His itchy feet could start up at any time. If he couldn't offer commitment then it wouldn't be fair to start anything with Rina. She deserved more than a brief affair. He wished things could be different—that *he* could be different—but he was too much of a realist to believe they could.

He needed to keep a physical distance from her. He made a quick decision to suggest a number of temples as their next stops. As always, Rina's notebook was out almost immediately. She lost herself in her drawings, ignoring all the noise and bustle around them.

When the heat of the day became a little too much for them, they managed to catch the late-afternoon show at Jawaharlal Nehru Planetarium.

Being pressed close to Rina in the darkness, under a vast, brightly lit sky, was like being alone in their own universe. He glanced over at Rina to see whether she was feeling the same intimacy, but she was watching the presentation in fascination. He laughed at himself, slightly put out that she didn't seem affected.

When they came out, Rina was buzzing. 'That was incredible!' she said.

He nodded.

'At first I wasn't sure, you know,' she continued. 'I never thought space and the solar system would be that interesting, to be honest. But those images. The lights. I wish there was a way I could incorporate some of that into our products.'

Connor's lips turned up at the corners. 'I'm sure you'll find a way,' he said, with absolute conviction. 'I think your problem is more likely to be how to narrow down which ideas you start working on first.'

'You've got that right,' Rina said. 'There are so many bubbling in my mind. I want to try everything immediately. But I'll need to get my aunt to approve any new work.'

'You still haven't heard from her?' he asked, almost wishing he hadn't when her shoulders slumped and she shook her head.

It was clear Rina loved her aunt. It must have been hard for her to leave against her wishes.

'Your aunt will come around,' he said. 'And maybe this experience, and seeing how happy you are after travelling, will help her realise you needed to get away and how good it's been for you.'

'Maybe.' She didn't sound as if she believed it.

'You mentioned her concern is a result of your accident? Now your aunt will know that you can travel alone without anything bad happening.'

'I guess... I just wish she would take some counselling to help her manage her anxiety. I would love to travel *with* her.'

'Did you have counselling?'

'Yes, for years after the accident. Have you ever spoken to a therapist about your childhood?'

'No, but I've encouraged my brother and sister to take therapy when they feel they need it. Our childhood was far from ideal and they suffered a lot.'

'It sounds like you suffered as well. Perhaps you should consider counselling too.'

He nodded. It seemed natural for Connor to discuss personal, intimate topics with Rina. He'd shared more details of his childhood with her than her had with anyone—even Nihal or Rohan. And he'd shared his feelings about it. Something he never did.

The following day they went out to KR Market. Rina seemed to be in her element among the different flowers and plants, taking photos and making more notes.

'This is so wonderful! This place! This

whole visit! I'm almost tempted to take Nihal up on his offer,' she said.

'What offer?'

'Nihal said if I was ever interested in working on product development in one of the Newmans labs he would make it happen.'

'And are you interested?'

Rina laughed. 'I could never leave my aunt or my lab at Lachance Boutique. It's my baby.'

Connor laughed too, but he was reminded again of why they could never act on the attraction that had been between them since that first day. Rina might want to leave her own backyard occasionally, but at the end of the day her home was with her aunt in Switzerland. His home was in England. And if he got the promotion to Global CEO he could choose to remain in London. He had no intention of moving—even the idea of it brought up childhood memories of packing his suitcase every few months.

'Are you okay, Connor?'

His brow creased. 'I'm fine—why do you ask?'

'I thought you shuddered? Are you cold?'

He shook his head. He hadn't realised his body had reacted physically to the idea of moving—proof that it wasn't in his future.

After they'd left the market, Connor noticed Rina's gaze following the autorickshaws as they passed by.

'Do you want to ride a tuk-tuk?' he asked.

Her eyes became bright with excitement at the possibility. How did she find such joy in the little things?

'But what about the car?' she asked.

'We can either ask the driver to meet us somewhere, or send him home for the day.'

'Oh, let's send him home for the day. He's been more than patient with us. But will we see him again before we leave?'

'Yes, he'll be taking us to the airport.'

'Okay. That's good. Because I wanted to give him a small gift along with his tip.'

Although the tipping culture was common, Connor was touched by how Rina wanted to go that extra step and give him a thank-you gift too. And if he knew Rina the way he was sure he did, the gift would be personal. She'd chatted enough to their driver during their trips to have an idea of what he and his family needed.

They used a tuk-tuk for the rest of their visits.

Already having to sit close to each other because of the narrowness of the vehicles, they found the unsteady surfaces jostled them together constantly. Feeling Rina pressed up against him wasn't helping Connor in his resolve to ignore his attraction to her and remain detached. Was she feeling the same desire, the same need to press even closer together? He could hear her breathing accelerate and deepen with every contact.

Back at the hotel, he walked her to her room. She inserted her key card, but before she unlocked the door she turned round to face him.

'Thank you. For today. And for yesterday.'

'You don't have to thank me. I was happy to go with you.'

'That's not what I meant.'

He bent his head, but said nothing.

She reached up and placed a gentle kiss on his cheek. He reached out his finger to trace it across her hairline, as if moving an imaginary stray strand. Bending down slightly, he pressed his lips to her cheek, then slowly moved across, pressing another kiss to the corner of her mouth. Neither of them seemed to breathe as their heads turned and their mouths met, slowly and gently at first, then becoming harder, hungrier, as they were both swept up by the smouldering heat.

He was in danger. In danger of giving in to this desire and taking everything she was offering—taking their physical attraction to the next level. In danger of wanting more from her than the physical—of wanting everything.

He dragged his mouth away before it was too late.

CHAPTER ELEVEN

RINA WAS RELIEVED when she found out she wasn't sitting next to Connor on the plane to Mumbai. Having a single seat next to the window was a luxury she hadn't expected. The only downside was that it gave her time alone with her thoughts. Still, it was better than sitting in close proximity to the very subject of those thoughts.

When they had finally broken apart after their kiss Connor had blinked rapidly, looking startled. He'd mouthed goodnight and then walked away. She'd watched him, her heart leaping when he'd turned around to look at her before quickly turning back when he caught her gaze.

But this morning he'd acted as if nothing had happened. As if they hadn't shared the most amazing kiss ever. Yet again.

They wouldn't get a chance to speak to each other during this short flight from Bengaluru to Mumbai. Although she didn't suppose that either of them would have brought up the subject of the kiss even if they had talked. But she replayed it constantly in her mind.

Had it really been that amazing, or was her memory hyping up something fairly normal?

At the end of the day, it was only a kiss. It didn't mean anything. It couldn't mean anything.

They only had a few days in Mumbai before they flew to Frankfurt, and then a night in Frankfurt before they drove to Lake Thun. After that there was a good chance she wouldn't see him again, depending on whether she was able to influence Aunt Maria to accept Newmans' proposal on her own or whether she would need to liaise with Connor to convince her.

From the moment she'd first seen Connor she had been confused about what kind of relationship she wanted with him. Initially, she'd thought it could be a friendship, but her physical attraction to him hadn't decreased and she'd started hoping they could have a romantic relationship too. All that had changed when she'd found out he was Newmans' representative—but that was before she'd come up with the deal to convince Connor to take her to India with him.

And Connor hadn't always been able to maintain that professional difference. He'd shown her in the way he looked out for her, in the way he always thought about what she would find interesting, even though he gruffly pretended they were only in India to visit the company offices. He'd even arranged this detour to Mumbai, and taken more leave. Was it any wonder she liked him so much?

The problem was she could easily feel so much more for him, but it would be futile when they wanted different things. She *had* to push away any inkling that she was falling deeper. She already knew she cared—a lot— but she had to protect herself from passing a point where her heart would be too far gone.

Newmans had arranged for a car and driver to be at their disposal in Mumbai, even though they wouldn't be in the city for business. Rina knew they were pulling out all the stops to encourage Lachance to licence Essence, but it still made her feel like a princess, with all her whims catered to.

At her request, their first stop was at the Gateway of India.

'Why did you choose to come here first?'

Connor asked as they stood in front of the basalt memorial arch.

'I don't know,' she answered honestly. But Connor's kind and caring but curious expression encouraged her to try to articulate her thoughts. 'I guess I've been thinking about identity a lot recently. And this symbolises an important part of India's history. I haven't learnt much about it and I want to start changing that. Particularly since I'm actually British but I don't feel at all British. I've lived in Switzerland the majority of my life, but I'm not sure how Swiss I feel either. I've felt closer to my mum since I've been here. Would I have felt closer to her if I'd stayed in England?' She shrugged. 'I don't know. I'm just rambling now.'

'Not rambling at all—processing. It's a complicated issue. I understand something about the need to feel a sense of belonging.'

'You do?'

He nodded. 'Not about family or nationality. But, growing up, I didn't ever make any attachments to people because we moved so often. London's my home now, and it's the first time I've felt settled.'

Rina's widened her eyes at hearing him share such vulnerabilities with her. 'You mentioned before that your family moved a lot because of your father…'

Connor's smile was grim. 'As I told you, my dad never stayed in one job for long, so we had to move wherever he could get work. To be honest, I don't think he tried. Dad would get bored if we stayed in one place for more than a few months. We could always tell when he was beginning to get restless and a move was imminent.'

After hearing about his family life she could understand why he wanted to be settled in one place. She reflected again on how different they were in what they wanted for the future. She wanted to explore more of the world, but now it made sense why travel was only a necessary evil for Connor.

'Sounds like your dad has a wandering spirit—like me,' she added after a pause.

He glanced at her sharply. 'Wanting to see the world isn't a bad thing. Particularly when you're young and don't have any commitments. But it's a different story when you have a wife and three children you're dragging around with you.'

'Didn't your mother try to give you a stable home base?'

His laugh was humourless. 'My mother is

perfect for my father in that respect. She loves moving around...never putting down roots.'

'Roots are important.'

It was strange how close she felt to him in that moment. Was it odd that in some ways she envied Connor's parents? They'd each found a partner who shared the same vision. She and Connor might not have a future together, yet they shared a need for belonging that had been shaped by their childhoods.

Automatically she put her hand in his, and then suggested they continue walking along Marine Drive. She considered taking a ferry to Elephanta Island, to look at the caves, but when Connor told her he had something planned for after lunch she decided she didn't want to risk running late for whatever it was.

Despite her constant questions, he refused to tell her where they would be going, not giving her any details. She could barely sit still during lunch as he teased her, by pretending to drop hints about the activity, making her guess random places, and laughing at her face when she got it wrong.

'It's probably going to be a big let-down,' she said finally, sitting with her arms folded and her jaw jutting out.

'Probably,' Connor agreed placidly. 'But if

you don't like it's only a couple of hours out of our lives.'

'But you *do* think it's something I'll like?'

She sighed with frustration at his enigmatic smile.

'It can't be somewhere I've mentioned I'd like to visit because I didn't know we'd be coming to Mumbai until the last minute.'

'You really are impatient.'

'I've decided I don't like surprises.'

He laughed. 'You would hate it if I told you now—especially now that I've built up all this anticipation.'

She grinned, acknowledging the truth in what he said.

'Come on,' he said, once they'd finished eating and paid for their meal. 'We should head back to the car. It's quite a distance.'

'Is it?' she said, her ears perking up. 'So are we going outside Mumbai, then?'

He tapped her nose affectionately. 'It won't be long until you find out. Let's go.'

Rina remained silent, smiling to herself, not only because of this surprise trip Connor had planned for her, but because after they'd left the restaurant he'd voluntarily reached for her hand and held it as they walked to the car.

She loved these small indications from Connor that he cared about her—not as a business partner, but as someone he could be fond of if he allowed himself.

Her head drooped. How often did she have to remind herself it didn't matter whether Connor opened himself up to the possibility of something developing between them—*she* couldn't allow it. She might be having a taste of independence and exploration, but after this was over she would return to Lachance tower and stay there with her aunt.

As the car arrived at their destination, Rina read the large words on a sign.

'Bollywood?' she asked.

'That's right. We have a tour of Bollywood Park and Mumbai Film City.'

'You're kidding? That's incredible! Is it a real set?'

'As far as I'm aware. We'll find out on the tour,' he said.

But Rina was already looking things up.

'It says there are permanent sets of a temple, a prison, a court and even an artificial waterfall. And they're used by a lot of the Bollywood films. Wouldn't it be great if we got to see someone filming using one of the sets?'

She'd mentioned that she enjoyed watching Bollywood movies in passing, in a general conversation about films, and yet—as she'd come to learn was typical of Connor—he'd remembered that detail and organised a visit he thought she'd enjoy.

She couldn't believe her luck in meeting such an incredible man. She would be foolish to let these few days be all the time she ever spent with him. She resolved to do everything she could to convince Connor to stay in contact with her once he was back in England and she was back in Switzerland. She might be a naïve optimist, but perhaps if they stayed in contact they could at least be friends. And maybe one day the stars would align and they could find a way to have something more.

She didn't want their inevitable goodbye in a few days to be final.

After they'd finished their tour, they went out for dinner and then walked along Marina Drive, which looked vibrant and magical in the night-time lights, before returning to the hotel.

Outside her room, Rina paused to thank Connor again. They stared at each other intently, their breathing becoming shallow. She wasn't sure who made the first move before they were devouring each other. He pressed kisses across her cheekbones, then along her jawline, before she impatiently brought his mouth back to hers.

She was about to invite him into her room when he broke away and hurried off down the corridor. She tutted in frustration. Each time they were affectionate he bolted, as if he was…

She paused, trying to analyse Connor's behaviour. He ran away as if he was scared of what had happened. He couldn't be scared that she didn't want their kisses—she'd obviously been a willing and eager partner. So what was he so afraid of? Could it be that he was frightened of his feelings for her? Was he beginning to drop his guard? And did that mean she had a chance to break down his remaining barriers?

She would just have to try harder.

She couldn't help chuckling as she walked over to the windows of her hotel room. She felt as if she was reliving her teenage years, being walked home after a date and sharing a goodnight kiss, counting down the minutes until they could see each other again and kiss once more.

Of all the places Rina could have suggested they visit in Mumbai, why had she chosen to come to the Dhobi Ghat first thing in the morning?

Connor watched as Rina scribbled away

in her notebook, wondering what could have inspired her just by watching linen being washed. Was it the sounds or the colours? Since Rina was a scientist, creating hair products, perhaps it was the soap.

He would love to talk to her more about her work and her ideas. She was so passionate about everything. It was a shame she couldn't share such an important part of her life with him. But he completely understood about her concerns over proprietary information, so he'd avoided asking her anything at all.

He was unsure why he kept forcing himself to draw boundaries around his interactions with Rina. It didn't seem to do any good anyway. They'd kissed a few times now. And every time it became harder to walk away. He wanted to indulge their passion. But he had to leave.

Suddenly Rina snapped her notebook shut and walked over to him.

'All done?' he asked.

She nodded.

He no longer wanted to pretend he had to interest in what she was working on. It was her choice how much she shared.

'Were you thinking about soap?'

'Hmm…?' Her attention had been taken

now by the linen being hung out on the lines to dry. 'Soap? No—why?'

He shrugged. 'I was trying to work out what caught your interest.'

'Oh, I was watching the dhotis work. The different techniques they use.'

He grinned. 'Did it inspire you to come up with an alternative to the lather, rinse, repeat process?'

She giggled. 'Some things are too perfect to change. It wasn't the process itself I was thinking about. It just gave me some ideas about something we're working on back in the lab. I can't wait to share it with my colleagues.'

'It won't be long now.'

Rina grimaced. 'I'm looking forward to seeing Aunt Maria and getting back to work, and I haven't felt that way in a long time. But I'm sad we're leaving India. There are so many places I haven't been yet.'

'Now you've come away for the first time, perhaps your aunt will be more open to you travelling in the future.'

'I truly hope so,' Rina replied with a sombre tone. 'In my ideal world I would travel abroad at least twice a year, so I can come back to India annually and then for the other time I would pick a different country each time.'

'What's stopping you?'

'Apart from my aunt? Work... Finances...'

'You do realise if you manage to influence your aunt to accept Newmans' proposal then once the deal is finalised you're going to be very wealthy, don't you?'

He almost burst out laughing when her jaw dropped.

'I never even thought about it.'

'Well, start thinking about it—and all the potential travelling you'll get to do.'

'I don't think so,' Rina replied with a sad shake of her head. 'Aunt Maria hasn't replied to any of my messages. She's really upset. I can't imagine she would be happy with me travelling again, and I don't want to disappoint her.'

Connor squeezed her shoulder, then couldn't resist running his hand down her arm to join their fingers.

Rina shrugged. 'I guess the memories of this visit will have to be enough to last me a lifetime.'

Connor's eyes widened. Memories would have to be enough to last him too. If he got the promotion this would be the last time he travelled for business, and travelling for pleasure wasn't likely for him.

Now the prospect was in front of him, he

wasn't as pleased as he probably would have been before meeting Rina. Seeing the sights with her had been fun. This time around, travelling hadn't brought that clenched feeling to his stomach at the notion of living out of a suitcase. In fact, he was the one who'd brought up his childhood, almost wielding it like a shield against falling for Rina.

But in the end how he felt about travelling didn't matter. He was still the same man who was incapable of making a commitment—he still couldn't offer her anything approaching a relationship. Hurting Rina was the last thing he wanted to do. He wished he could be a better man than he knew he was, but pretending he could change would inevitably lead to disappointment.

'Where do you want to go next?' he asked as they walked back to the car.

'I'd like to go shopping.'

'To a street bazaar?'

'No. Can we go to a mall? I don't mind which one.'

Connor raised his eyebrows. 'A mall?'

'Why do you sound so surprised?'

He shook his head. 'No reason.' He gave the driver their destination. 'Is there something specific you want to buy?'

'No.'

'Are you researching which hair products are stocked there?'

Rina furrowed her brow. 'I hadn't thought of doing that. I just want to do some window shopping.'

'I see...'

Why was he so surprised by her choice? It wasn't because she wanted to shop—there was nothing unusual in that. And it had been surprising when she'd suggested Dhobi Ghat in the morning. Maybe because they were both public places?

After their kiss the previous night, Connor would have chosen to go somewhere peaceful, where they could talk easily. Or he would have chosen to stay in his hotel room with her.

On second thoughts, a public place like a busy shopping centre sounded like the perfect choice.

They held hands as they walked around the mall, as if they were the same as countless other couples there.

But they weren't a couple.

He didn't know what they were.

He didn't know what he was doing.

If he were sensible, he would release her hand and keep some distance between them. Even though his gaze went to their joined hands, the instruction from his brain didn't make it to his hand, as if it had been interrupted on the way. Perhaps by his heart.

He stopped suddenly. Rina gave him a questioning look, glancing at the store they were passing, which happened to be selling luggage.

'Do you need to replace your suitcase?' she asked.

'No. I need the restroom,' he replied—untruthfully, but he needed some space to get his thoughts in order, and that excuse was the best he could come up with at the time.

He stood at the washbasin, running some water over his face.

Why was he thinking about his heart? His heart knew as well as his head that there was only goodbye in their future.

So why was he holding her hand? Why was he kissing her?

What impression was he giving her? Did she think they were starting something?

He had to let her know the reality of the situation. He wasn't going to lead her on or make promises he couldn't keep.

There was never any point in his forming an attachment because he never wanted to make a commitment when he knew he couldn't maintain it. And even if he were foolish enough to ignore his previous experience and try a relationship, Rina would be the wrong person.

It wasn't even about the travel, per se. It was the fact that she'd been sheltered most of her life and she needed to be free to live a little—just as she'd said when they'd first met.

He couldn't restrict her, and he'd already seen how much it had irritated her when he'd worried about where she was going and whether she was alone. Once, she'd described herself as a wandering spirit, and that was how he saw her—a free spirit, full of optimism, looking for the best in the world, the best in people.

He was too cynical to believe the best of people. He never wanted to be the cause of Rina's spirit being trapped and creating her disillusionment because sometimes—more often than not—things didn't work out simply because you wanted them to.

They needed to have a serious conversation. He would have to apologise if he'd given her the wrong idea.

He debated suggesting they return to the hotel, but decided it would be better to have this conversation in a public place. Not because he didn't feel it deserved privacy, but because he couldn't trust himself if they were alone in a hotel room together—not when there was a bed in the room, and not when the sensation of holding her in his arms, pressed tight to her, was almost physical rather than a memory.

'Why don't we get a drink and maybe some kulfi?' he asked. 'I think we should talk?'

Rina furrowed her brows, then shrugged. 'Sure. Let's find somewhere we can sit down.'

Once they were seated, he fiddled with a sugar packet.

'What's wrong, Connor?' she asked.

He took a deep breath. 'I think we need to talk about our kiss last night.'

'And the other nights?' Rina added, with raised eyebrows.

'They were very pleasant,' he said, with considerable understatement. 'But I don't want you getting the wrong idea. We can't start anything.'

'Why not?'

Staring into her deep, dark brown eyes, he wasn't sure of the answer. 'Geography,' he finally managed to say.

He saw the look of determination in Rina's eyes and knew their conversation was far from over.

'We live in different countries,' he added.

Rina quirked an eyebrow. 'And no couple has ever tried to make it work long distance?'

He snorted. 'I've never made a *close*-distance relationship work,' he told her honestly. 'I wouldn't have high hopes of making a long-distance one work. I didn't see the point of them when I was growing up and I don't see the point of them now.'

He knew he should say something callous, almost deliberately mean, to convince her there was no future for them, but he couldn't bring himself to do it. He never wanted to see that kind of pain in her eyes—it was the reason he wasn't prepared to encourage whatever was happening between them. He couldn't hurt Rina.

But if she was upset now, because of their conversation, it was better than the potentially greater hurt a little further down the line, when he lived up to his nature and was unable to make a commitment to her.

'It's not just the distance,' he went on. 'You want to explore the world and I don't enjoy travelling.'

'I understand that. But I don't know how much travelling I'd get to do, and you wouldn't have to come with me.'

'I don't want to hold you back from your dreams of seeing the world.'

'I can have new, different dreams.'

'I would never want that. It wouldn't work

out between us. You told me you want to get married some day, and I never want to settle down.'

'I also said I thought it was unlikely that I would find someone.'

'Because of your aunt. Because of geography. It all comes back to that.'

She furrowed her brow. 'You're not prepared to hear anything I have to say about this?'

'I'll hear you. I'll listen to your opinions. But they're not going to change my mind, no.'

CHAPTER TWELVE

THE FOLLOWING DAY Rina stared out of her hotel window at the view of the River Main. She was in Frankfurt, but somehow the excitement of being in a new city was missing,

She wasn't sure whether it was because it was the last day before they headed home to Lake Thun, or because of her sobering conversation with Connor at the shopping mall.

They hadn't spoken much on the flight from Mumbai. She'd still been feeling emotionally fraught, and had decided to escape into the colourful and joyful world of one of the Bollywood inflight movies, enjoying it even more after their visit to Film City.

Connor had his laptop out, so she presumed he'd been working—as usual.

Perhaps he was tweaking his proposal for Lachance. She was mindful that if Connor had his way, the only reason she would have anything to do with him in future would be if she persuaded her aunt to accept Newmans' deal—an added incentive for her to work her influence, even if she wasn't already convinced it was the best path for Essence.

It was frustrating, how he'd couched all those reasons why they couldn't be together as if they were for her benefit. Although she accepted there was a lot of truth in what he said, she didn't agree that it had to be an all-or-nothing situation. There had to be room for compromise. But she didn't have long to find one.

She headed down to Reception to meet Connor, as they'd agreed. Part of her didn't want to go sightseeing with him—not after their conversation. But if she refused to go out or went alone she'd be doubly spiting herself, not only missing out on exploring a new city, but also missing out on spending time with Connor. And the more time she spent with Connor, the more likely she would be able to find that compromise solution.

Why couldn't it be like in novels, where all the rooms in a hotel were booked for a convention, or something, which meant she would be forced to share with Connor. Although in that scenario Connor would probably hire a car and drive them straight back to Switzerland, so on reflection she decided it was better the way it was.

As they walked along the river, Rina's hand almost instinctively sought out Connor's, but at the slightest brush of her fingers he moved away. She shoved her hands into her jacket pockets to stop her reaching out to him again.

She tried to convince herself that was a good sign. If he really had drawn a line under their relationship he wouldn't have any problems with the occasional touch. But it was awkward. She couldn't even find something to chatter about, small talk seemed futile.

Connor didn't say anything either. She would hate it if having that frank discussion had ruined the core connection she'd always felt between them. She didn't want potentially their last moments together to be spent in silence.

To ease the tension, she paused along the way to take some photos, smiling ruefully when a man offered to take their photo together. Connor met her smile, as if he too remembered their day on the Sigriswil Panoramic Bridge. Had it really only been two weeks ago?

As they posed, Connor put his arm across her shoulder, as he had before. This time Rina wasn't going to miss out on the opportunity, and she put her arm around his waist.

It felt so right to her, standing so close to Connor. Couldn't he feel that too?

She raised her head and met Connor's stare. He turned towards her slightly and reached out to run a finger along her cheek. She leaned in towards him...

She didn't know whether he would have leant down to her, because they were interrupted by their amateur photographer, returning Rina's phone to her.

Her heart did somersaults. He wasn't indifferent to her. He might be giving mixed signals, and his body was probably acting against his will, but she would take that as a sign that he instinctively wanted to be with her.

'Do you want to visit the shops or a museum while we're here?' Connor asked, moving ahead.

She wasn't surprised. Connor was an intelligent man. He would have realised what his action meant. Her positivity went up a notch or two.

'I don't, really. I'm happy just walking around and seeing what there is. Is there somewhere you want to go?'

Connor shook his head. 'I'm happy to walk around too.'

They moved on. Rina almost stumbled when she felt Connor's hand against hers. She tried not to grab it too enthusiastically, or clasp it too hard, but she wasn't going to give him a chance to let go.

After a leisurely walk, they reached Main Tower.

'You know, this is one of the stops for the hop-on, hop-off bus tour of Frankfurt,' Connor said.

'Is it?'

'I happen to have tickets for the tour bus, if you want to go on it?'

Rina smiled. 'You do?'

Connor gave an embarrassed shrug. 'I arranged them at the hotel. I thought it would be an easy way of getting around the city. I don't think we have too long to wait for a bus, if you're interested.'

'Sure—why not?' Rina replied.

They chose to sit on the top deck of the open-top bus. The weather was comfortable for mid-October, but a stark contrast to the heat and humidity of India.

Rina snuggled up to Connor, pretending she wanted him to keep her warm. He moved his arm around her, hugging her close to him.

She grinned. Intellectually, he might not think their relationship was a good idea, but instinctively he wanted to be with her as much as she wanted to be with him. There *had* to be a way to get him to change his mind about them.

If he'd made it clear that he wasn't interested in her, she would never have considered pursuing him. But he'd admitted he was attracted to her and enjoyed her company. He was letting geography and a belief that he didn't 'do' commitment keep them apart. And that didn't make any sense. If Connor was always there for his siblings, and had maintained long friendships with Nihal and Rohan, then he *could* do commitment.

But there was no point saying that to him—she had to make him see it and believe it.

After a full day of sightseeing, Connor and Rina returned to their hotel to freshen up before dinner.

They'd had such a lovely time together, but now it was coming to an end. She didn't want to say goodbye, although she accepted it was inevitable. It broke her a little that she hadn't found a way to convince Connor.

She'd never felt this way before.

She loved him.

She wasn't going to deny it to herself. Her

feelings for Connor had always been strong, because she'd been falling a little more in love with him every moment since they'd met.

He was and would always be the love of her life. Maybe her dream of marrying one day would never come true, but there was still one dream she could make happen—there was still one memory she wanted to make.

Nodding her head with determination, she left her room and walked along the corridor to Connor's.

His eyes widened with surprise when he answered her knock, but he gestured for her to come inside.

Barely waiting for the door to close, she took a deep breath. 'Connor, I have something I need to say to you.'

'Go on…' he replied.

She couldn't work out whether his expression was curiosity or wariness.

This was it. Her last chance.

'I know everything you're saying is right, Connor. I know we don't make sense together in the long term. I know you think what I want is completely the opposite of what you want. I know you don't see me as part of your future. And I accept that. But I don't care.'

Connor blinked a couple of times and shook

his head, as if trying to clear it of what he'd heard. 'I… I don't know what you're saying.'

Rina swallowed, then she clenched her fists, gathering her strength. 'I know you don't think we have a future together. I'm not asking for that. I'm not asking you to make any commitment, or any promises to me. I'm asking you for one night. Just tonight.'

Just tonight.

Connor kept repeating the words in his head.

Could she really be offering him a one-night stand.

Could he refuse her if she was?

'Rina…' he began, trying to be sensible.

'Don't say no, Connor.'

Rina shook her head and walked closer to him. He took a few steps backwards until the side of the bed hit his legs, causing him to sit down.

'Rina…' he said again, with a quiver in his voice as she put her arms around his neck and pressed her lips against his. 'Rina, we can't do this.'

He felt bereft when she moved away.

'Why not, Connor? Why can't we have tonight? One perfect night and then we'll say goodbye.'

'Do you think you could say goodbye easily afterwards?'

She laughed—a low, sultry sound that speared right to his groin.

'You seem very confident about your abilities, Mr Portland. Now I definitely need to see if you're right.'

He couldn't help laughing. 'Rina...' he said, holding her against him and then pulling her onto his lap.

The sensible voice inside his head was telling him to move away. But when she looked at him through half-closed lids and smiled, before brushing her lips along his jawline, he found it hard to pay any attention to that voice.

Just one night, he thought, before laying Rina down on the bed and covering his body with hers.

Hours later, Rina cuddled into Connor's side. He couldn't resist bending his head to taste her lips again, and both of them were quickly swept up by passion once more.

Then Rina's stomach rumbled.

They both laughed at the sound, finally breaking their kiss.

'We should get something to eat. What time is it?' Connor said, reaching for his phone.

'It's after nine-thirty. We could get Room Service, or take a walk by the river and see if anything's open.'

Rina stretched, and at that moment all thought of leaving the bed fled his mind.

Until Rina's stomach rumbled again.

'Come on. Why don't we have a quick shower and then go out.'

Rina raised her eyebrows. 'You want us to shower?'

Connor bit his lip at the image that formed in his mind. 'Not together. We'll never leave the room if that happens.'

'I'm not sure that's the punishment you think it would be…'

'Come on, Miss Lachance. Go to your own room and get ready.'

'Okay,' Rina agreed putting her clothes back on. 'But this,' she said, pointing at his bed, 'is to be continued.'

She wasn't going to get any argument from him about that.

They walked hand in hand along the river, tracing the same path they had taken that morning. But it felt different now. Now he was feeling relaxed. Happy. He couldn't remember the last time he'd felt this level of happiness—if he ever had before. When was the last time he'd felt so at peace?

Rina was a special woman. A spark of light that he hadn't realised he needed in his life. But she needed more than him. He couldn't change who he was for her, and he would never ask her to change for him. Which left them at the same impasse as before.

He'd learnt when he was young that good-bye was an inevitable part of life. And if you didn't get too attached, it wasn't even difficult to say.

If tonight was all they would have together as a couple, then he would enjoy every moment of it.

Rina had taught him to make the most of any situation, and that was exactly what he was going to do.

CHAPTER THIRTEEN

RINA WASN'T SURE why she was so reluctant to return to the tower. Was it worry about her reception from her aunt? Or was it the inevitable moment when she would have to say goodbye to Connor?

They had spent one perfect night making love. Rina had hoped that would be enough—that the memories of their intimacy would be enough to last the rest of her life. But now she couldn't deceive herself. They would never be enough.

The drive to Lake Thun seemed to go too quickly. By unspoken agreement they talked about a variety of topics, but nothing too personal—nothing about the future.

She was grateful Connor had insisted he drive her back. He could easily have taken a flight to London directly from Frankfurt. Instead, he would be staying overnight in the same hotel he had on his previous visit, before driving to Geneva and taking his flight home.

She'd asked for one night. But had she truly meant that? Or did she want more?

She wasn't sure if spending another night with Connor later would help, or make it even harder to say goodbye.

She turned her head to drink in Connor's profile. He must have sensed her looking at him, because he turned and smiled.

'Are you ready to go home?' he asked, reaching out to squeeze her hand.

'Quite honestly, no,' she admitted. 'Once I go home my adventure comes to an end. And I still don't know what kind of reception I'll get from my aunt.'

'Do you want me to stay around for a while?'

She shook her head. 'I think it's better if I see her alone.'

They completed the drive in silence, with Rina still worrying about how her aunt was going to react.

Connor dropped her off outside Lachance tower, then drove off to check in to his hotel.

Rina took a long breath, squared her shoulders and prepared to see her aunt.

Her aunt completely ignored her. All Rina's attempts to start a conversation were futile.

After a couple of hours, Rina followed her

aunt into the lounge, then barred the door to prevent her aunt from leaving the room.

'Aunt Maria, please talk to me,' she pleaded.

'Why do you want me to talk to you? You didn't care about my opinion before you left. I don't understand why you came back. Why didn't you keep travelling?'

'I'm ready to work again. I just took a short holiday. I needed inspiration. I was stagnating. My work was stagnating.'

'Well, I wouldn't want that to happen again.'

Rina closed her eyes, desperately hoping the words to appease her aunt would come to her.

'I have so many new ideas to share with you. Why don't I take my bags to my room and then, when I come back down, I'll make us something to eat and I can tell you all about them.'

'Why are you telling me? I have no say over what you do, apparently.'

Rina huffed, but decided there was no point replying to her aunt when she was in that mood. It wasn't the first time her aunt had been like this, but it had never lasted for so long before.

She went to the room that had been hers since she was ten years old. Although she loved the circular tower room, even one wall could be constricting if it was all she could see.

Now she'd had her first adventure, and although she hated being on poor terms with her aunt, Rina couldn't regret making the decision to go.

Not only had it been the correct decision for her, she was also convinced that accepting Newmans' proposal was the best decision for Essence.

She had a large arsenal in her power, to use to convince her aunt to make the deal—assuming her aunt was ever ready to listen to her. Essence actually belonged to her. As she'd told Connor, when she'd been trying to convince him to take her to India with him, she didn't fully understand the legalities, but she had created the formula for Essence, and the method of extraction, so she'd have a large input into the final decisions concerning the future of Essence in particular.

What had happened between them didn't change their business relationship—particularly since he had made it clear he wasn't interested in any other kind of relationship with her.

She went into the kitchen to start preparing dinner. She didn't really expect her aunt to come and chat with her, as she usually did, but she couldn't help being upset.

Then she received a text from Connor, telling her he was waiting in the field where they'd first met.

She rushed out. His broad smile when he saw her momentarily lifted her spirits and she ran into his open arms.

'What's wrong?' he asked as she held tighter to him.

She looked up at him without releasing her hold. 'Nothing. Don't worry.'

She felt his chest heave underneath her cheek.

'Is your aunt upset with you?' he asked.

'You could say that.' She gave him the gist of what had happened.

He took a sharp intake of breath as he held her closer. 'Is it because of Essence? She doesn't want to sell?'

'It's not about that at all. It's because I left. She didn't say it explicitly, but I know she was worried the entire time I was away—even though I left her messages and she could have spoken to me at any point if she'd wanted to. I've always understood she lost everything in that one accident, but is it really so selfish that I grabbed a once-in-a-lifetime opportunity?'

'You're the least selfish person I know.'

Her lips quirked. 'You're a little bit biased.'

'Do you want me to speak to her?'

Rina was confused. 'What good do you think that's going to do?'

Connor shook his head ruefully. 'I don't know, but I feel helpless seeing you so upset when I can't do anything.'

'You're doing everything I need just by listening to me. It means a lot to have someone to share my thoughts with.'

Rina frowned as Connor took a step away.

'You should think about *all* your alternatives,' he said, staring at the view of the mountains rather than at her.

'I don't understand what you mean?'

'I'm sure you and your aunt will fix things, and you'll go back to your former relationship. But working at Lachance Boutique isn't your only career option. I know many companies would snap you up. Nihal wasn't joking when he offered you a job. And you would get to live in a different country.'

Rina swallowed the lump in her throat. 'I could never leave my aunt—you know that.'

'Your aunt will always be your family. But she doesn't have to be your employer too.'

'Despite how things are between us at the moment, with my holiday and my preference to accept Newmans' offer, I know it would break Aunt Maria's heart if I went to work for a different company. I couldn't betray her by leaving for good.'

Connor inclined his head to acknowledge what she'd said. Then he spoke. 'I'm just saying you shouldn't let anyone tie you down and force you to settle down before you're ready. Not your aunt…' his voice trailed away but she knew what he was going to add '…and not me.'

He had physically distanced himself. Was he worried that she was hoping their relationship would continue? She couldn't pretend she wasn't holding on to that hope.

She walked over to the fence and looked out at the view of fields and peaks in the distance. She understood the parameters Connor had set, and she accepted them, but it wasn't wrong to be hopeful, was it?

Perhaps a tiny part of her had hoped Connor would ask her to go to London and stay with him—but she knew that wasn't really ever going to happen. Although a woman could always dream…

She still didn't even know whether he intended to keep in touch with her outside of business. He'd initially been clear that there couldn't be anything more between them.

And then they'd kissed.

And then they'd made love.

But in the end, despite their current frosty relationship, Rina needed to stay with her aunt. She owed her everything. And Connor wouldn't move from England.

It didn't matter how much she cared about him, or how much he cared for her, there could never be anything lasting between them.

These two weeks were all there would be, and the memories would have to be enough for her.

But she still had a few hours before Connor was leaving Switzerland. And her problems with her aunt would still be there after he'd gone.

She didn't want to waste a single minute.

She led out her hand to Connor. 'Come on,' she said. 'Let's go back to your hotel.'

CHAPTER FOURTEEN

CONNOR WOKE EARLY the next morning and lay on his side, watching Rina as she slept. For a moment he imagined what it would be like if he could wake up to the same view every morning. But he knew it was impossible.

Nothing had changed—not materially. Their relationship might have developed into a physical one, and he was no longer going to deny he cared about Rina—a lot. But the fact remained that they wanted different things out of life. And there wasn't any space for compromise—not that he could see anyway.

He knew she would never leave her aunt permanently, but he'd watched her revel in the taste of freedom she'd had the chance to experience. Her relationship with Maria would soon settle back into its loving nature, but she had grown—he'd observed that himself in the time he'd spent with her. Soon her wings would take her to so many new places, and she would meet so many new people that she would grow beyond him.

So today they would say goodbye.

He sighed and lay back on the bed with his arm bent beneath his head.

He was used to saying goodbye. This shouldn't be any different.

But he knew it was. They weren't saying goodbye because they didn't like each other. If they had been any other two people they could probably have tried to find a way to make things work. But she was Rina Lachance, genius inventor, the wunderkind with wanderlust—someone who shouldn't be held back in any way. And he was Connor Portland, product of a nomadic childhood, a loner outside his family and a few friends— people who'd refused to accept his determination not to form attachments.

In a way, Rina was similar to those friends. She'd listened when he'd explained why they couldn't be together. She hadn't tried to persuade him to try having a relationship. But she'd also refused to accept that meant there couldn't be anything between them, and she had claimed one night with him.

And then another night.

What would he do if she wanted more? Would he be able to refuse? He hadn't stopped desiring her. He hadn't stopped wanting her. He hadn't stopped caring about her.

But it would be kinder in the long run if he broke off all contact with her now.

How long would they really be able to maintain any sort of relationship? Hopefully, she would be travelling, and if she wasn't travelling she would be here with her aunt in Switzerland. They would hardly get a chance to meet up since he was also likely to be busy.

He really hoped Rina would be able to influence her aunt to make the decision to agree to Newmans' proposal. And if Lachance did sell the licence for Essence, the role of Global CEO was his. The promotion he'd been working towards for ages. The culmination of years of hard work. He should be excited that it was almost his. Instead, he had a sense of regret...

When he dropped her outside Lachance tower later that morning, she lifted her head and opened her mouth. He shook his head before she could say anything, and bent forward to kiss her on the cheek. Then he got straight back into his car and drove away.

This time he couldn't even say goodbye—it was too hard to speak.

It felt like a physical pain, watching as her figure grew smaller in the rear-view mirror.

* * *

It didn't take long for Connor to realise he'd made the biggest mistake of his life. It had only been a few weeks since he'd left Rina at Lachance tower, but he missed her.

Of course he missed her kisses, and the feel of her in his arms, but he'd expected that. What he hadn't expected was how much he missed seeing her bright eyes and the huge smile he couldn't help responding to. He missed her laugh. He missed making her laugh. He missed talking with her, hearing her thoughts. He even missed sharing his own thoughts.

He hadn't made any attempt to contact her since he'd left. But then she'd made no effort to contact him either. Would it be strange if he messaged her out of the blue? What would she think? Would she be pleased?

He knew there was only one way to find out, so he sent her a text. Almost immediately he received a response. They exchanged a few more messages, but it wasn't enough for him. He video-called her.

Her smiling face coming into focus warmed his heart. It was exactly what he needed to see.

'Hey, congratulations, Mr CEO,' she said, in greeting.

'The promotion hasn't formally taken place yet.'

'But that's all it is? A formality.'

'How are things with your aunt?' he asked.

Rina grimaced. 'Still not good. She speaks to me about work matters, but she always makes these snide comments about when I'm planning to leave the tower. You know, if I hadn't inherited half of the tower from my dad, I think she would ask me to leave.'

He furrowed his brow. 'I'm sure it wouldn't really come to that.'

'She said she doesn't want to hear my ideas at all. And she's said I'm not needed in the lab for a while. Almost like I'm re-placeable.'

'Perhaps she needs more time. Why don't you go travelling again?'

'Not sure it's a good idea to leave her again when that's what's annoyed her.'

'She might need to be reassured that you'll always come back to her and that you'll be safe.'

Rina nibbled her bottom lip, making him groan inwardly—he knew she didn't intend it as a provocative gesture.

'Do you really think so?' she asked.

'I do. She's worried about you.'

'I know. And I don't like worrying her. But one positive thing from all this is that Aunt Maria mentioned she's finally started seeing a counsellor.'

'I'm pleased.'

He was telling the truth. Rina's openness about her own therapy had made him think about whether speaking to someone would help him.

'I hope it helps her,' he said. 'But you can't wait until she's ready. Do you really want to stay stuck in your tower?'

She shook her head. 'Actually, Mausami has contacted me, asking if I want to meet her in Japan in a couple of weeks.'

'You should go.'

For the first time in his life, Connor wished he could travel…with her. It didn't feel as if he was living out of a suitcase when he was travelling with her.

'I don't know…'

'Go. Your aunt will be fine. She'll miss you a lot, though.'

'Will she?'

'Of course. *I* miss you.'

Her face brightened at his words. 'I miss you too.'

'Do you want to video call again, later in the week?'

She nodded vigorously.

For the next few months Connor and Rina had regular video calls. She often showed him the view from her hotel rooms as she travelled, even showed him some of the sketches she'd made in her notebook.

He looked forward to the nights when he would get to see her beautiful face appear on his screen. But it wasn't enough. He needed to be in the same country—he needed to be in the same room.

And *he* was the only reason he wasn't with her. *He* was the obstacle to his own happiness.

He'd taken the plunge and started meeting regularly with a counsellor to help him process things from his childhood. There was still a lot of work to do, but he'd already seen how he'd let his fear of forming attachments, of making commitments, stop him trying to make it work with the woman he loved.

He'd known on a subconscious level for months that he'd fallen in love with Rina— perhaps even at first sight, even though that still sounded unbelievable. Definitely he had by the time they'd got to Mysuru.

And that was what made it different from the past. He'd never loved any of the women he'd dated before, so of course he hadn't wanted to commit to them. With Rina he wanted attachment, he wanted commitment...he wanted for ever.

He wanted to spend a few more months working with his counsellor, but he was already starting to make plans for a future with Rina.

And one of the first people he needed to speak to was her aunt.

CHAPTER FIFTEEN

RINA WALKED THROUGH the old town towards Charles Bridge. It was her last day in Prague. She was flying back to Switzerland the following day, and was more than ready to be back home with Aunt Maria.

The last six months had been wonderful. After meeting up with Mausami in Japan she'd visited Singapore, and then returned to Switzerland where she remained, determined to stay at Lachance tower and wait until her frosty relationship with her aunt melted.

It didn't take long. She'd proved to her aunt that she could travel safely and that she would always return home. And, on top of that, some of the ideas she'd been inspired with on her travels were shaping up to develop into exciting new products.

After Rina had been a month at home, her aunt had actually suggested she travel to Italy to inspect some potential suppliers.

Rina understood what a big step that had been for her. She'd never forgotten why her aunt was so protective of her. She was her aunt's world, and Rina would never downplay the love Aunt Maria had surrounded her with. And it was a testament to that love that Aunt Maria was now accepting Rina's need to spread her wings.

For the past six months Rina had travelled on business every couple of weeks. She suspected her aunt was going a little overboard in accommodating Rina's wanderlust. But now she was itching to spend a long time in her laboratory, testing out her theories and refining new products.

She still wanted to travel in future, but she didn't have the same sense of longing to get away she'd used to have. And she could definitely appreciate why Connor hadn't enjoyed all his business travel.

There was a pang in her chest when she thought of Connor—as she did constantly.

She'd been over the moon when she'd received his first message, two weeks after they'd said goodbye. Although she'd been the only one who'd actually *said* goodbye. Connor had left without even a wave.

Since then they'd kept in touch, and video called at least once a week. He seemed to enjoy hearing about her travels, but he had never invited her to visit him in London. She didn't really know what to make of that. Only last month she'd brought up the suggestion herself, but he hadn't sounded keen, mentioning something about him being very busy for a while.

She'd had to take that at face value—she had no reason to doubt what he said. But although she often mentioned how he might join her, he hadn't taken her up on her offer—which she understood, knowing how he felt about moving from place to place.

But surely he couldn't still think geography was a barrier against them continuing their relationship?

Trying to sort things out over a video call or a message was never going to work. Once she'd settled back home she would book a ticket to London for a weekend. She had to see Connor. She missed being next to him, touching him, kissing him. She missed everything about him.

She'd fallen in love with him so quickly, part of her had wondered whether it was their proximity that had fed her emotions. It hadn't taken long after he'd left for her to recognise that her feelings for him were deep and strong and unwavering.

She loved him. But she'd never told him. She'd been too scared. And he probably hadn't been ready to hear any declaration earlier. But she could tell from their conversations that something was different about his views of the future.

She wanted to see Connor when she told him she loved him for the first time. Even though she had no expectation that he would reciprocate, she didn't want to deny her feelings.

But if he cared about her at all—as she was sure he had started to—then she wanted to discuss how they could work on a long-distance relationship. She was ready to do all the travelling, so he never had to move or feel as though he was living out of a suitcase.

And although, for now, she still couldn't leave her aunt permanently, she could fly to London to spend weekends with him, if he agreed.

She couldn't wait to finish this next appointment so she could go back to her hotel and call Connor. She wanted to hear his voice and see his smile.

She checked her watch. She was still early for her appointment with a potential supplier of glass containers for their products. For some reason he'd suggested through his correspondence with her aunt that they meet at the Charles Bridge, although she'd told her aunt to tell him she was happy to find his shop. Apparently he'd been insistent.

She shrugged. Perhaps his goods were as quirky as he sounded.

She hoped the meeting would go quickly. Another reason Rina wanted to get back to Switzerland was because she was sure something was happening with the Essence deal. Her aunt had been in negotiation with Newmans, but neither she nor Connor had spoken about the deal. All Connor had told her was that he'd stepped away from the deal, feeling he now had a conflict of interest.

And here she was, back to thinking about Connor again. She needed to put him out of her mind and concentrate on Lachance Boutique— for the next couple of hours at least.

But first she needed to find this person she was supposed to be meeting next to the statue of St Christopher. Rina wondered whether Aunt Maria had deliberately chosen the patron saint of travellers for their meeting spot.

She was staring at the statue when she heard a familiar voice behind her, calling her name.

She turned towards the sound, wondering whether her longing had conjured the voice.

She blinked a couple of times to make sure she really was seeing the man she loved most in the world right in front of her.

'Connor!' she cried, almost running in her hurry to get to him, to hold him in her arms and reassure herself that he wasn't a figment of her imagination.

'Rina…' Connor said, as he pulled her to him and swept her off her feet. 'Rina, I've missed you.'

'I've missed you too. I've missed you so much. I can't believe you're here,' she said, cupping his face in her hands and then lowering her head to plant hundreds of kisses on it. 'This is the most wonderful surprise,' she said when they finally broke apart. 'I can't believe Aunt Maria helped you.'

'Maria thinks I'm great.'

Rina raised her eyebrows at Connor's use of her aunt's name. In the past he'd referred to her formally as Miss Lachance.

'Shall we walk along the bridge?' he suggested before she could ask him any more about her aunt.

'Okay… We can head to my hotel, if you want?' she said shyly, biting her lip while she waited for his response.

'Sounds good,' he said, holding out his hand. She turned to him as soon as they were in the lift going up to her room. 'I was going to fly to London to see you,' she said.

'That would have been a waste of time,' Connor replied.

'What?'

She took a step back. What did he mean by that? Didn't he want her to visit? To spend time with her?

The lift came to a stop. Once they were inside her room she moved slightly away from Connor.

'Why would me coming to London be a waste of time, Connor?'

He shrugged with one shoulder. 'Because I won't be there.'

She raised her brows. 'How do you know? I didn't tell you when I was planning to go.'

'That's not the point.'

She sniffed. He was hiding something from her, and it was aggravating the way he was stringing out the conversation.

'Why don't you want me to come to London, Connor? Just tell me the truth.'

'Because I don't live there any more.'

'You've moved?' That was the last thing she'd expected to hear.

'Yes, I moved to a town near Lake Thun a few weeks ago.'

Rina's mouth dropped open and she fell into a nearby armchair.

Connor laughed at Rina's shocked expression. Her surprise at seeing him on Charles Bridge was nothing compared to her reaction at this news.

'Are you serious, Connor?'

'I wouldn't joke about it. I moved to be closer to my girlfriend?'

'Me?' Rina asked, somewhat foolishly, pointing to herself.

'Of course you,' he replied, rolling his eyes.

'But why? Why would you move for me?'

'I love you,' he answered, as if it were the most obvious thing in the world.

She drew in a sharp breath. 'I love you. I have for a long time—although I only realised the truth in Frankfurt.'

Connor felt the warmth of true happiness spread throughout his body. It had been enough for him to know he loved Rina. He had hoped over time her feelings for him would become stronger and she would come to love him too. He had never dared to hope she already did.

And her revelation that she had known in Frankfurt made her actions in coming to him and asking for that one night even more special.

'Come here,' he said, pulling her up and into his arms.

They kissed deeply. He desperately wanted to make love to her, but they still had lots to talk about first.

He sat down, drawing her onto his lap. 'You can't leave your aunt,' he said, 'and I can't be without you. So the simple solution was for me to move.'

'Connor, I can't ask you to give up your need for stability.'

'You're not.'

'You can't know that!'

'Rina,' he said, holding her face in his hands. 'You don't need to worry. Actually, I took your advice and started seeing a counsellor. I'm going to continue, but it's already helped a lot. He's helped me understand how all my life I've thought that belonging meant to a place. That moving constantly meant I never really had a home. You made me realise home isn't a place—it's a person. Wherever you are is my home. And although I can't promise I'll always travel with you, I will go occasionally. And when you go without me I'll always be at home, waiting for you.'

He noticed Rina blink rapidly, but she couldn't stop the tears falling.

'Don't cry, my darling,' he said softly, wiping the tears with his thumbs.

'I'm just so happy. It doesn't feel real.'

'Should I pinch you?' he offered, smiling. She nodded.

'I think I'll kiss you instead,' he said.

When they finally came up for air, his ever-practical Rina asked, 'But what about your job? What about Newmans?'

'I resigned.'

'What? Aren't you the Global CEO?'

'They offered the promotion to me. I turned it down. I'm after a new challenge.'

'What kind of challenge?'

'I've found a small company with an amazing product developed by an intelligent, beautiful woman. It needs some help with growing the business, and I have some expertise in that. So I've accepted a job with Lachance Boutique.'

'My aunt offered you a job without telling me?'

'She told me she's in charge of recruitment.'

'She is, but…'

Connor grinned. He'd finally seen Rina at a loss for words.

'Are you pleased?' he asked.

'I think so… There's a lot to process. So we'll be working together?'

'That's right. Although I'll have nothing to do with the product development side.'

'Don't you think you might get bored with me?'

Connor laughed. Didn't she know every day with her was a new delight? 'Impossible!' He kissed her again.

'I love you, Connor Portland.'

'And I love you, Rina Lahiri Lachance.'

EPILOGUE

RINA SIGHED DEEPLY as she lay in the field of rampion and gazed up at the cloudless sky. She'd had another frustrating day in the lab, and Lachance Boutique hadn't launched a new product in almost a year.

The products they had developed since her trip to India had gone on to be extremely successful globally, with Connor's expertise at the helm. And Essence was performing wonderfully with the new distribution agreement Connor had negotiated with Newmans, which had brought the product to a wider market at a lower cost, leaving strategic control to Lachance—everything she'd wanted for her miracle product.

But although she could rest on her laurels, she had no intention of doing so. Not now Lachance Boutique was hers completely.

Less than two years after Connor had joined the company, her aunt had surprised them all by announcing her plans to retire and cruise around the world. She'd transferred ownership of the boutique to Rina, but wanted to keep her share of the tower—which Rina had been happy to agree to.

At the time, Connor and Rina had been planning their wedding. Rina had known that although Connor was happy to live in Switzerland, he missed his family and England. So, since Aunt Maria was the only reason Rina stayed in Switzerland, she'd suggested they move to England.

They'd appointed an operations manager to look after the company in Lachance tower, then bought a home outside London and set up an office for Lachance Boutique nearby.

Their visits to Switzerland coincided with Aunt Maria's trips back—which was the reason they were staying at Lachance tower now. Rina had hoped working in the tower would bring her some much-needed inspiration. But it hadn't happened so far. Perhaps it was time for her to go on her travels again. She hadn't been for a long time…

'Ma! Ma!'

Two young voices called out for her—the reason she hadn't gone off on any inspiration trips.

She sat up to watch her three-year-old son

and daughter running towards her, gathering them in her arms as their momentum pushed them all backwards. She gave them a quick tickle, enjoying their high-pitched squeals. Having twins was rewarding, but it was also exhausting.

Rina couldn't pull her eyes away from her husband, now walking towards them. Her heart still flipped at the sight of him, the same way it had when she'd first seen him six years before.

She and Connor had only been married for a few months when they'd found out about her pregnancy. Rina had initially worried that the news, coming so soon after settling into a new job and getting married, would be too much for Connor. He'd had to go from being a man who avoided attachments and commitments to having the biggest commitments of all thrust upon him. But it turned out she'd had nothing to worry about—he cherished fatherhood as much as being a husband.

'Ma, will you read this story, please?' her son asked, resting his head against her legs.

'Please, Ma,' her daughter echoed, right on cue.

She looked at the book, which contained their favourite story, *Rapunzel*. She raised her eyebrows at Connor.

He put both hands up. 'Don't blame me. I've already read it to them three times today.'

'Yes, but Daddy's not good at being the witch like you are,' her daughter explained.

'I'm not sure if that's a compliment,' Rina said, laughing.

Connor sat behind her, drawing her to him. 'Well, I did tell them you cast spells in your magical tower,' he said, against her ear, pressing a kiss to her temple before sitting back.

Rina rested against Connor, with her children resting against her. Could anything be more perfect?

She opened the book and started to read.

'Daddy said there's a plant called Rapunzel,' her daughter said when she'd finished.

'That's right. It's also called rampion.'

'Is it really what Rapunzel's mother wanted to eat?' her daughter asked.

She nodded.

'That's funny…naming your baby after some food,' her son remarked.

'If we'd named the two of you after what your mother ate when she was pregnant you'd be called idli,' Connor said, poking his son's belly gently. 'And you'd be called dosa,' he continued, poking his daughter in the same way.

Aunt Maria called the children to her, leaving Rina and Connor alone in the field.

'So, will you be eating authentic idli and dosa soon?' he asked, lifting her hair, which she hadn't cut since India, and kissing the back of her neck.

'What do you mean?'

'You're planning your next trip.'

'How could you tell?'

'The look on your face before the children came to you.'

She pulled his arms tighter around her, covering his hands with hers. 'I was thinking about it.'

'We can find a good time for you to go. I'll take care of the kids. And perhaps later in the year we can all go on holiday as a family.'

Rina closed her eyes and lay back, basking in the sun and in the comfort of Connor's arms.

* * * * *

If you enjoyed this story,
check out these other great reads
from Ruby Basu

Sailing to Singapore with the Tycoon
Cinderella's Forbidden Prince
Baby Surprise for the Millionaire

All available now!